NO LONGER PROPERTY OF
SEATTLE PUBLIC LIBRARY

the PROM

a novel
based on the hit Broadway musical

by **Saundra Mitchell**

with **Bob Martin, Chad Beguelin, and Matthew Sklar**

PENGUIN BOOKS

PENGUIN BOOKS
An imprint of Penguin Random House LLC, New York

First published in the United States of America by Viking,
an imprint of Penguin Random House LLC, 2019
Published by Penguin Books, an imprint of Penguin Random House LLC, 2020

Copyright © 2019 by Chad Beguelin, Bob Martin, and Matthew Sklar

Penguin supports copyright. Copyright fuels creativity, encourages
diverse voices, promotes free speech, and creates a vibrant culture.
Thank you for buying an authorized edition of this book and for
complying with copyright laws by not reproducing, scanning, or
distributing any part of it in any form without permission.
You are supporting writers and allowing Penguin to continue
to publish books for every reader.

Penguin & colophon are a registered trademarks of Penguin Books Limited.

Visit us online at penguinrandomhouse.com.

Based on the Broadway musical The Prom.
For more information, visit theprommusical.com

LIBRARY OF CONGRESS CATALOGING-IN-PUBLICATION DATA IS AVAILABLE.

Paperback ISBN 9781984837547

Printed in the United States of America

1   3   5   7   9   10   8   6   4   2

Set in Jenson Pro   Book design by Mariam Quraishi

This book is a work of fiction. Any references to historical events, real people, or
real places are used fictitiously. Other names, characters, places, and events are
products of the author's imagination, and any resemblance to actual events or
places or persons, living or dead, is entirely coincidental.

The publisher does not have any control over and does not assume
any responsibility for author or third-party websites or their content.

I love you, Mommy.

Thank you for giving me the world.

— SM

Broadway Score! scores a chat with Dee Dee Allen and Barry Glickman on the set of their new show, *ELEANOR!*

(cont. from page 2)

Glickman and Allen invite me into the inner sanctum, backstage at the Alliance Theatre. There are signs of the show in production everywhere. A row of foam heads sports the steel gray wigs and dental prosthetics Allen wears to transform herself into Mrs. Roosevelt, and of course, FDR's wheelchair sits in a corner, its seat taken by a cigar (real) and a pair of glasses (prop). Despite the serious subject matter of the show, Drama Desk winner Glickman and Tony winner Allen are all laughs with each other—and us.

BS!: What does it mean for one of Broadway's grand dames—

BG: I guess this question is for me, Dee Dee!

DA: Just try to cut me out of the spotlight, honey!

[We laugh and rephrase.]

BS!: What does it mean for *two* of Broadway's greats to come together on a show like *ELEANOR*?

DA: I truly feel like I'm changing lives. Don't you, Barry?

BG: Indeed. I've come to realize that there's no difference between a celebrity and the president of the United States.

DA: By the time I get tuberculosis in act 2, even the people who are dead inside will be on their feet.

BG: And knee-deep in tissues! If the audience doesn't leave depressed, we haven't done our jobs.

DA: It's power. Literal power.

BG: Not to quote a certain show that destroyed a producer, a pop star, and a comic book hero—but with great power comes great responsibility.

DA: And I think we're great enough to handle it.

If FDR Could Stand for This, He Wouldn't

. . . Dee Dee Allen inhabits Eleanor Roosevelt in the same way a demon inhabits the monstrous Annabelle doll from the self-titled horror film series, but with less grace and charm. Allen doesn't so much present the first lady's activism to the audience as she shoves it down their throat: a Molotov cocktail of American flag soaked in syrup and set on fire.

One would think next to Allen's shrill, scene-chomping antics that Glickman would offer a respite. One would be wrong. Glickman's FDR just might be the most insultingly misguided and offensive performance this reviewer has had the squirming misfortune to endure. The aging Glickman has none of the former president's fire or finesse, and the actor's attempt at a mid-Atlantic accent is so laughably lost, it lands somewhere west of New Jersey.

If you were considering buying a ticket, do yourself a favor. Find a way to contract tuberculosis instead. It's a terrible way to go, but worlds better than watching this Eleanor hack herself to death in slow motion.

1. Edgewater, Indiana

EMMA

Note to self: don't be gay in Indiana.

Actually, that's a note for everybody else. I'm already gay in Indiana, and, spoiler alert, it sucks.

I told the internet before I told my parents—on my You-Tube channel, Emma Sings. It's me, my guitar, and mostly cover tunes of whatever's popular at the moment. People leave more comments if you sing songs they know, and I like that. I don't have a lot of friends, so those little digital hellos make me feel less alone in the world.

I'm not trying to get discovered or anything like that. First, that literally never works, and second, the idea of fame terrifies me. I already feel like everybody knows my business. Of course, that's because they actually *do* know my business. One slip, and it was everywhere.

So, this is what happened.

Picture it: the summer before freshman year. Picture me: mousy and shy, with thick-rimmed glasses that give me owl eyes. I'm at a youth group picnic hosted by the Vineyard, which is a church. You know, one of those new churches with branding and youth pastors with drum kits.

They really tick off churches like First Lutheran and Missionary Free Baptist and all the other traditional places of worship packed into Edgewater, Indiana. The cheesy signs in front of them that used to say stuff like WHAT'S MISSING FROM CH CH? U R! started to get very snarky when the Vineyard opened.

Naturally, this means all the teenagers want to go there. High-level rebellion, right? *No, Mom, I'm going to the cool church, where I can wear jeans during the service!* And naturally, this means that all the youth group invites that used to lead to punch and cake parties in dingy fellowship halls suddenly lead to big outdoor picnics that still feature pretty unfortunate food, because it's still a church pitch-in.

That's how I end up with a plate of mini meatballs in barbecue sauce. I've heard too many horror stories about potato salad and egg salad and macaroni salad and basically any salad that uses mayo as glue, and I've also read that baby carrots are rejected regular carrots that are bleached and shaved down, so those are also a big no.

A Crock-Pot full of steaming hot meatballs doesn't exactly say summer fun (maybe in Sweden?). But the contents seem safe. I loaded up on them, but now I'm trying to figure out how to eat them without making a mess. These things are impervious to plastic forks and knives, which is what I have on hand.

There's a line at the food tables, and I don't really care to stand in it long enough to get a spoon. Also, I kind of don't feel like drawing attention to myself by cutting in line with an excuse, *Oh, I just need a spoon!* Even extremely adorable people get side-eye for jumping ahead in the food line at a church potluck-slash-picnic, and I'm awkwardly cute at best.

Additionally, who eats meatballs with a spoon? Meatball Spooner wouldn't be the first name people ever called me, but in this moment, it feels like it would be the worst.

Spoiler alert: it's not the worst. But I'll get to that.

So, I'm standing there, trying to ninja food into my face, and *she* walks up. Wavy auburn hair, bronze skin, dark eyes, and she stops. I stop. The world stops. Probably the universe stops; I can't explain the physics of it.

I can only explain the magic, because in that moment, Alyssa Greene looks at me and turns into a goddess. A brilliant, kind, smart, funny goddess in shimmery lip gloss that I suddenly want to taste.

You guys, I'm not surprised to find myself hard crushing on Alyssa Green. I've always liked girls. I was once a teeny, baby lesbian. In sixth grade, I was crazy into Madison from *Talk to the Hand*, and *not* because I wanted to be her friend. And now, I'm a regular, teen-sized lesbian. I have thoughts about Ariana Grande (impure thoughts), and I feel like if I could meet Lara Jean of *To All the Boys I've Loved Before*, I could help her start the sequel, *To All the Girls Who Eclipsed Them*.

But I *am* surprised when Alyssa reaches past everybody at the dessert table and presents me with a giant skewer. With a blinding smile, she says, "This is the only thing that works."

I'm not surprised that she's nice, but that she noticed me. That I'm somehow actually visible to the most beautiful girl ever to breathe air. The surprises keep coming, because she touches my hand. And stands with me while I impale meatball after meatball. She even lets me share one with her. RIGHT THERE. AT THE CHURCH PICNIC.

On the lawn, people play cornhole—which is legitimately the name of a bag-tossing, target-hitting game—and Christian rock blares from a speaker, courtesy of Pastor Zak's iPhone playlist. The sky is endlessly, perfectly blue, and Alyssa Greene puts her phone number into my phone. Then she makes me text her, so she has my number, too.

That night, I recorded a TSwift cover for Emma Sings. Everything inside me was so fantasy and cotton candy that I told the world I was in love with a beautiful girl without a thought. Without the slightest hesitation. I uploaded, I picked a cover thumb that looked semi-decent, and I went to bed.

My mother woke me up.

I'm sure one day this will be a hilarious story, but she shook me awake and shoved a printout of my YouTube page into my face. And when she demanded, "What is this?" all I could say was, "I don't know!" because I didn't!

"We didn't raise you like this!" she yelled.

"Like *what*?!" I asked, because again, literally woken out of a dead sleep with a piece of paper crammed halfway up my nostrils.

My mother rose up to her full, not all that impressive height of five foot four. "You know exactly what I'm talking about, Emma."

But I didn't! They didn't raise me to . . . sing on the internet? Post videos in the deeply awesome salmon jammies my nan got me for Christmas?

I mean, to be fair, after a couple of seconds, the old brain kicked in. Last night, I posted a video full of shameless, unfiltered heart-eyes for a girl who'd given me a marshmallow skewer. (And an extremely passable rendition of "Our Song," if I do say so myself.)

And after I'd posted, someone in town must have watched it and—their delicate sensibilities inflamed—immediately informed my mother. (Mom printed out my profile page like it was a recipe for Crunchy Ramen Noodle Salad; there's no way she found it on her own.)

And in that moment, I guess I was too stunned to be scared of my parents, whom I knew, for a fact, to be lifelong members of a church that officially hated gay people but in practice was "too nice" to say anything about it in public. I must have taken silence for approval, which historically has been an extremely bad policy position. So I told the truth.

"I just like her," I said.

"Well, you can just stop," she snapped, as if I could cancel the gay like Netflix. "Not in this house! Not under my roof!"

If this were a heartwarming, *Chicken Soup*-y kind of story, this is the part where I'd say, yeah, it was hard for a while. But eventually my parents remembered that I was their precious only child, and they loved me unconditionally. They joined PFLAG and started wearing really embarrassing T-shirts at pride parades that said FREE MOM HUGS and FREE DAD HUGS. I brought my girlfriend home, and by graduation, they'd stopped calling her my "friend."

Sorry. Your soul is going to go unsouped this time.

They argued about it for weeks: conversion camp or eviction. And ultimately, they let me take my guitar and my school stuff, reclaimed my key to the house, and kicked me out. All my clothes, my laptop, the box of birthday cards I'd saved since I was six—well, I heard they burned what they couldn't donate. What a couple of drama queens, right?

So now I live with my grandma, Nan, two blocks from my parents' house, in Edgewater, Indiana. I'm the only out queer kid at school, and it's a good thing I still have my YouTube channel.

It's aggressively ordinary, and I know I'll never go viral. But I do have subscribers, and their responses feel like friends. Like-minded, queer friends. I need them. I need them so desperately, I treat it like QUILTBAG Pokémon: I gotta catch them all.

There are places where it's in to be out. New York, San Francisco . . . imaginary places, in imaginary lands, far, far away from here. But Indiana is not one of those places. So yeah, that's my advice to you: don't be gay in Indiana, if you can absolutely help it.

There's nothing here for you but heartbreak.

2. Edgewater, Indiana

ALYSSA

You've probably never been here, so let me tell you, Indiana is a beautiful place.

Sometimes at night, the moon is so bright behind the clouds that the sky is pearl silk. I get up at five A.M. to go to school, and the roads are lined with silvery fog. Just before the sun starts to rise, as my bus makes a left onto State Road 550, everything turns purple, then lavender, then pink.

In the summer, we have acres of fireflies. There's a pond in the woods that's clean enough to swim in. Raspberries and mulberries and blackberries grow along fences, free for the taking. Come fall, we have a riot of autumn color and apple orchards where you pick your own. Have you ever had a piping-hot fried biscuit with apple butter? Deadly good.

We have the kind of winter you see on Christmas cards. Rolling fields, blankets of white, the whisper of snow falling, and nights so dark, you can see the Milky Way. On the clearest days, the fields drift on toward forever. It's a silvered, glittering expanse, stretched until it surrenders to an icy blue horizon.

Indiana is small towns, and Fourth of July parades, and basketball. A lot of basketball. Way too much basketball, actually. It's the state sport-slash-religion. If you make it to high school without swearing allegiance to the IU Hoosiers or Purdue Boilermakers, they throw you in a pit of voles for all eternity.

(Special dispensation given for the Fighting Irish; you're allowed to love Notre Dame, but you're also a little suspect.)

Supporting our school team, the James Madison Golden Weevils, is key in Edgewater. When we have homecoming, it's not for the football team. Nope. *They're* ranked third to last in the state; they're dead to us.

Homecoming is for the basketball team. The prom court is for the basketball team. The pep rallies, the bake sales, the wrapping paper sales, the industrial-sized-cans-of-flavored-popcorn sales, all dedicated to b-ball. Go Golden Weevils!

Consequently, the basketball team is the reason that prom tickets are strictly rationed. Between varsity (first through third strings), and junior varsity (two strings), and freshman prep (*four* strings!), we have a guaranteed hundred and fifty athletes, with a probable hundred and fifty athlete dates, and the fire marshal says we can't have more than four hundred people in our school gym.

Thus, when the Future Corn Keepers of America set up their table to sell prom tickets in the Hall of Champions (aka the front hallway with all the trophy cases), they have three essential items:

1. A cash box. This is a cash-only dance, and don't even try to bring a check from your parents. The

FCK spit on your mom's Precious Moments checks.

2. A stack of tickets designed by the one kid in school who knows how to use Photoshop well. (*Well* being the operative word; everybody around here knows how to filter for Insta, but when it comes to text, it's like a subreddit got font poisoning and started puking Papyrus and Comic Sans.)

3. The list. The list has two columns: Your Name. Date's Name. They are inextricably entwined; there are no stag tickets to our prom. The list is the reason why I've been having a serious discussion about prom with my girlfriend.

It's our senior year; this is our last chance. And I do, I really do want to go and dance under a cardboard moon and aluminum foil stars. I want to look into her funny hazel eyes that sometimes turn blue and sometimes green, depending on what she's wearing. I want to wrap my arms around her and let the whole world slip away.

But it won't slip away.

Not here. Not with my mom watching.

I want to make it clear: I'm not ashamed to be a lesbian. I love love, and I love my girlfriend. I love quiet murmurs and secret kisses. I love snuggling next to her on her grandmother's strangely velveteen couch, watching movies when the rain presses in from the west. I love that our hands are exactly the same size, but she has tiny feet with super long toes. When she sings, I love her even more. So much that it actually hurts, like there's a hand reaching in to squeeze my heart until it's a diamond.

She flickers like a firefly, because her hair is gold but almost brown; her eyes are blue but almost green. When she takes off her glasses, I like to press my nose to hers and just gaze in. It makes her laugh and blush, her cheeks suddenly pink as her lips. It's hard to whisper our love instead of shouting it to the skies.

But the thing is, my mother, she's not ready for it. She's fragile right now. She's *been* fragile since my father left. It was so easy for him. He just packed a gym bag and waltzed out into the night. Started a new family—well, based on when my half sibling was born, he started the new family *before* he walked out.

And since then, Mom has lived in this delicate crystal bubble. She thinks if she goes to church more, if she prays harder, if she cleans the house better, if she loses twenty pounds, if she raises me right, if she finally nails that pot roast recipe her mother-in-law gave her, Dad will come home. You can see the belief sparking in her eyes; she's a transformer hit by lightning. Everything pours out, hot and fast and endlessly.

That fire means I have to be the best daughter. My grades have to be all As, with weighted classes so my GPA breaks that 4.0 ceiling. My safety schools have to be other people's first picks. I have to teach Sunday school, and my kids have to have the best crafts, the ones that make their parents tear up at the preciousness.

But I'm president of the student council because *I* wanted that. Because I thought I could change things that needed to be changed and strengthen things that needed to be stronger. Still, I have to go to the prom in a lilac, spaghetti-strapped, knee-length dress that Mom worked sixty-hour weeks for a month to afford. It has Swarovski crystals on the bodice. Swarovski. Crystals.

And why? Well, she's the president of the PTA (remember: perfect in all things), and they're the chaperone hosts of the prom. This year *will* be perfect, and it will be perfect with me in *that* dress, on the arm of a boy in a tux.

Some boy. Any boy. Mom doesn't know who—but she sure has suggestions. Like Paolo, for instance, the exchange student who goes to our church. He's a real-life college sophomore and looks like TV sophomores look: cut and sculpted, walking with knowing hips. Don't get me wrong: he's hot. But he's also secretly sleeping with our choir director, so shhh, that's between us.

The point is, my mom's bubble is going to burst. She thinks she's working domestic magic, but she's really just lying to herself. Lying to the world. Any minute, everything is going to come crashing down on her. The spell will end, and I need to be able to put her back together again.

That's why I don't want to be the clock that strikes her midnight. And that's why I'm not-arguing-but-discussing-seriously the prom with my girlfriend. She wants one magical night, and I want that, too. But we live in Edgewater, Indiana, and signing that list with our names—Emma Nolan, Alyssa Greene—side by side, that's more than buying two tickets to the school gym.

Emma knows, better than anybody, how this story goes.

Her mom and dad still go to my church. Every week. Same pew. Same stony faces gazing up at the stained-glass Lord behind the pulpit. He gathers lambs at his feet; his hair is almost golden when the light streams through.

My dad's already gone. My mom's in la-la land, probably complete with magical dancing and show tunes. For me, saying yes to the prom is more than putting on a dress and buying a corsage. It's choosing to be the flawless, ideal daughter or to pick up a bat and shatter my mother into a million pieces.

And still, I want to fly free and say yes and kiss Emma under the glimmering light of a borrowed disco ball. So, we're discussing. Not arguing. I don't want to fight. It's spring and Indiana is beautiful again. Between us, and the blue skies, and the budding pear trees, and the tulips sending up little green tendrils toward the sun, I'm leaning toward yes. I want to say yes.

We'll see.

3. Subterfuge

EMMA

I have one hundred dollars in my pocket, but I'm not approaching the ticket table just yet.

I can't; Nick Leavel is putting on a production of *PROMPOSAL!* right here in the Hall of Champions. Standing room only, but mostly because it's the front hallway of a high school and nobody who values their life is going to sit on (a) the stairs or (b) the FCK prom-ticket table.

Excitement runs through the unwitting crowd. Nick has a brigade of junior varsity guys behind him. Carrying poster boards close to their chests, they have (what I'm guessing are) gas station carnations clutched in their teeth. Strobed out in sunglasses, his letter jacket, and *the* shiniest shoes I've ever laid eyes on, Nick puts two fingers in his mouth and whistles sharply.

Everyone in the Hall of Champions stops and turns. I kid you not, Nick pauses to take a quick gander at the gaggles who came to witness his wonder and glory. It's not enough for him to prompose to Kaylee Brooks, he has to make sure he's going all out. When you're the star center of the Golden Weevils, you have to shine.

"Kaylee," Nick says, taking her hands. He spins her around, and hilariously, he has to untangle their arms a little—he pretends it was all smooth. His slick dress shoes scrape against the floor as he turns to kneel in front of her. He looks up, but he doesn't say anything.

Instead, he nods and the junior varsity swoop in. Like, you can tell they've practiced this. Standing in a semicircle behind Nick, they drop the carnations at Kaylee's feet. And then, one by one, they flip the poster boards.

On the one hand, this is practiced and thoughtful and the tiny sliver of sentimentality lodged deep in my heart makes me smile. But let's be real, it's a bunch of tenth-graders fumbling with poster boards like it's a third-grade play about making flowers grow. Plus, it's happening in a high school hallway. In front of the yellowed JUST SAY NO posters. It's legitimately hilarious, but I keep my laughter to myself.

"Kaylee," the first JVer says, holding up his sign. It has a *lot* of writing on it, but helpfully for the audience, Nick reads it aloud. He literally glances over his shoulder to make sure he's in the right place.

Clutching Kaylee's hands, he says, "Girl," like he's a late-night DJ, "ever since freshman first string, everybody has been all up on this. You know I'm the OG around here, but it's lonely at the top."

My eyes roll so hard, I feel a little twinge before they roll back. Because, let me clarify for you: this OG is the whitest kid in our mostly white school. Light brown hair, pale blue eyes, he's the tallest, foamiest glass of milk in southern Indiana. Kaylee's lapping it up like a rescue kitten, too.

The next poster board falls, and I hover near the stairs because yes, I'm watching this, but no, I don't want to be caught watching this. As I cling to the straps of my backpack, I shiver suddenly. Not from cold, or excess cynicism—it's her.

When Alyssa gets close, I tingle everywhere. Everywhere. She doesn't stand *too* close, because nobody knows. But she's near enough that I catch a hint of the coconut oil she uses in her hair, the rich vanilla from her hand lotion, and if I'm making her sound delicious, well, obviously.

When Nick gets to the third poster board in his set (*Then something happened, girl, you turned my life around*), Alyssa murmurs to me, "Are you sorry we're not doing this?"

I muster a smile. "What, sonnets in the key of duh? Not sorry at all."

Her fingers brush the back of my arm, and she says, "You know what I mean."

Her skin is like silk on mine. I want to wrap myself in her, bury my face in the warm curve of her neck. I'd love to get on one knee for her, or write her a song and sing it from the balcony here at school. I really would. But it's easier to be sarcastic about something I'm never going to get than to admit that I want it. I'd go beyond big if Alyssa would let me. But she won't, so why think about it?

With a quick look back, I say, "I just want to go to prom with you."

"About that," she replies, and she already sounds like she's negotiating with Principal Hawkins for off-campus lunch for seniors. Not a promising start to a conversation I thought we were almost done having. She says, "I had a thought."

Welp. Time to pull down the metal shutters and chain off the old heart. Deliberately, I stare at Nick and his All-Star Carnation Revue, my brain full of Wonder Bread romance that they don't even appreciate.

Sure, yeah, Kaylee jumps up and down and makes Wookiee sounds before she says yes, and maybe Nick is into that. Behind her, her best friend Shelby pretends to be happy, but it's obvious by the way she stares longingly at her boyfriend, she's peeved this moment isn't hers.

But this is a show we've all seen before on YouTube, except with way worse production values. It's so *easy* for them that they don't even try. They don't *have* to try; people will remember this like a classic movie scene because it happens all the time in movies . . . for them.

I don't want my disappointment to come out when I answer Alyssa, but it might. My throat's so tight, I can't tell. "Let's hear this thought."

"We'll go together," Alyssa says diplomatically, "but let's sign up separately today. I need to be able to ease my mom into this. I think she's starting to come around."

I almost make a Wookiee sound of my own, and not a cute one. Baffled, I turn to look at her. "What's the difference between telling her today and telling her three weeks from today?"

"She's not ready yet, and you know she has this place on lockdown," Alyssa says. "If we buy tickets together, she'll know before I get home. I want to tell her. Present it exactly the right way, and that takes time."

The argument is there, and fair. The longer we wait to buy tickets, the less likely there will be tickets to buy. Since neither of us will be arriving on the underwhelming arm of a James Madison Golden Weevil, time is of the essence.

But, I point out, "I'm going to have to put down somebody's name. And you realize this means we're paying for two extra tickets we're not going to use. That's basically a gay tax."

"I'll pay you back," Alyssa says. She touches the back of my arm again, a secret touch no one should see because we're lingering under the stairs like bridge trolls. She swears, "I'll make this up to you."

Cash money is *not* on offer. Instead, it's everything. It's one night that's just ours, without hiding and sneaking and pretending we're something we're not. And I know it's hard—only out gay kid in my entire school, remember? And also the gay kid who didn't get to tell her parents on her own terms. And, *finalement*, the gay kid who lives with Grandma now. Truly, honestly, really, I get it. Lying about who you're with isn't quite as hard as lying about who you are, and yet . . .

"I just want to dance with you," I tell her, as I reach back and catch her hand, our fingers touching. For just a moment, she holds my hand, and we're together in the bright light of day. I see no one but her; I swear, I feel her heartbeat instead of mine. My lips sting for a kiss, but I let go before she can. Not here. Not now.

"Is that a yes?" she asks.

"Watch this," I say, some weird strain of bravado flowing

through me. I walk straight for the FCK table, because my thought is, I'm going to buy those tickets right now and show my girlfriend I'll do whatever it takes to have the most romantic night of our lives together.

Buuuut, I fail at the down low, because our star center just promposed, so of *course* all eyes are on the sign-up table as he pays for tickets while his girl watches, clutching a bouquet of sophomore-slobbered flowers. Now everybody's huddled around the table, buzzing about the spectacle, and *now* THE ONLY (OUT) GAY GIRL IN EDGEWATER just hopped in line.

The FCK doesn't care who buys prom tickets. They want their money (25 percent of ticket sales goes to their club to—I don't know—buy luxury pesticides or something), and my fee disappears into the lockbox before I can say hello. Breanna Lo slaps down two tickets, ready to inscribe my name and my date's name on them, while Milo Potts shoves the clipboard under my nose.

"Your name here," he says, tapping the first column. "Date's name here."

I say something really intelligent, like "Uh," then sign my name very slowly. I even say it out loud, as if Breanna might not know who I am. Emma Nolan, that's me, that's for sure, definitely write down *Emma Nolan* on that first ticket!

"Who are you going with?" Kaylee asks facetiously. This is quite possibly the first time Kaylee has spoken to me since ninth-grade English, when she asked me to trade seats because the fluorescent lights were, and I quote, making her eyelashes twitch.

Shelby perches at her elbow, Kaylee's perpetual garbage minion. "Yeah, who are you going with, Emma? I didn't know we had more than one lesbo in town."

This is when I want to look back. When I want to turn and see Alyssa standing there. The strength of her dark eyes would hold me up. We'd be connected; I wouldn't be alone. But that would be endlessly obvious. I can't do that to her. So I stiffen my neck like it's a vampire convention and stare at the blank line. Date's name. Date's name.

"You have to have a date," Breanna says curtly. The daggers in her eyes imply that I'd better not have just made her ruin a ticket for nothing.

"Your left hand doesn't count," Kaylee says. Nick snorts a laugh that makes me take back any benefit of the doubt I might have given him for his cheese-factory promposal. I'm also a big enough person that I don't stab him with the pen when he says, "Righty doesn't either."

Oh, the devastating wit.

Clenching my teeth, I scribble the first name I can think of, and it's not my fault I thought of it, it just happened. Here's hoping that the gathered brain trust isn't bright enough to make the connection. The only thing I can say in my defense is that she's a cute brunette and I have a type.

Kaylee reads over the top of the clipboard. "Anna Kendrick . . . son?"

"You don't know her," I mutter.

"Is she an exchange student or something?" Shelby asks.

"Sure."

Nick detaches his lips from Kaylee's ear long enough to

ask, "Then why don't you exchange her for a guy?"

With every bit of patience I have, I ignore them. I thrust my hand under Breanna's nose and say, "Tickets, please."

Kaylee all but falls back against Nick. "I can't wait to meet your really real gay prom date, Emma! Anna Kendrick . . . son sounds so *cute*. Doesn't she sound cute, Nick?"

He twines his arms around her, like she's bricks and he's ivy. The combined IQ is about right, anyway. With his chin resting on her shoulder, Nick nuzzles Kaylee's ear in a way that I find genuinely cannibalistic, then he spills a tanker's worth of smarm when he replies, "Not as cute as you, babe."

Without another word, I tuck the tickets into my backpack and turn. The smile I was about to shoot Alyssa dies. She's not even turned this way.

Her mother has appeared from nowhere, as she is wont to do. There are days when I see Mrs. Greene around here more than I see Principal Hawkins, which is saying something. She might be the slightest bit overinvested in all things Alyssa.

Mrs. Greene holds both of Alyssa's hands. I can tell they're talking about the prom, because Mrs. Greene keeps gesturing toward the table. The look on Alyssa's face is somewhere south of nauseated, but she nods. She nods and smiles and then takes one mechanical step in my direction.

There's a whole dance to being in and being out, and I know the steps. I'm supposed to disappear now. So I do, ducking my head and drifting past Nick's JV chorus line. They cough, "Gay, gay, gay," as I pass, and as Alyssa passes me, she says nothing.

Escaping, I chant back to myself, *She's worth it, she's worth it, she's worth it.*

4. Strategic

ALYSSA

I think—no, I know—I am the worst person in the world.

Mom shows up at school far too often these days, and this was the positively worst time. I didn't hear what Kaylee and her crew said to Emma, but I saw the look on her face. Her heart-shaped, freckled face, her face that I love more than any other face in the world.

When I have to pretend we're not together, it's like giant hands reaching down to break me in two. I feel the break, right in the middle of my chest. It exposes my marrow and my nerves, and I'm nothing but a walking wound.

"What's all that about?" my mother asks sharply. As we walk around Emma, we both hear the JVers barking, "Gay, gay, gay."

They do it to Emma sometimes, like it's supposed to be an insult. I guess they think it *is* an insult, instead of a statement of fact. Most of the time, I say something. But most of the time, I don't have my mother frog-marching me up to the prom-ticket table.

I swallow my anger, my frustration, my embarrassment. I

push down the hurt I feel because I can't say anything, and the shame that I don't. I put on my perfect-daughter smile and shake my head like it's light and worry-free. "No idea. Wow, a hundred dollars. I don't know if I have—"

Five twenties fan out in my mother's hand. She's so proud; she hands it to Milo. "I've got that covered. And now, little missy, you have to give up this big secret you've been keeping."

Pinned to the floor in a panic, I say, "I'm not keeping any secrets!"

With a practiced, carefree laugh, my mother plucks the clipboard off the table and a pen right out of Milo's hand. With a flourish, she fills in my name, then fixes me in her gaze. "Your date, sweetheart? You've been talking him up, and now it's time to reveal all."

My hummingbird heart beats so fast, it feels like it's stopped. I *have* been talking up my date. Very carefully, without pronouns. *I think you'll like my date, Mom. My date's so brave, so talented, so cute. You're definitely going to meet my date soon.* But I am not prepared to come out in the middle of the Hall of Champions, in front of Kaylee and Shelby. They have the biggest mouths in James Madison. They do *not* get to see my mother break. This will *not* be the next group-text intrigue.

"John," I say finally. What a nice, generic name. What a nice, nobody-you-know kind of name. Except my mother's brows are arched; they're question marks. That presses some primal button in me, the big red one that says, *Answer her right now or ELSE!* Stunned, I hear myself say, "Cho."

Oh no. I just told my mother I'm going to the prom with hot Sulu. My face stings; I wait for her to bust me. Instead, she simply lights up and scrawls his name beside mine. She doesn't suspect a thing, because she asks with quiet delight, "How do we know John Cho?"

My blush deepens, but I keep it together. "Model UN. I met him at Model UN. He was Australia."

"Oooh," Mom says, pretending to fan herself. "He comes from a land down undah, does he?"

From the weird accent to the expectant way Mom looks at me, it's like I'm supposed to get something out of it. Well, what I get out of it is that I just set my plan to ease Emma into my mother's sights back by three weeks, easily.

Why did Mom have to be here at this exact moment? Why couldn't she just stay at work and phone in her school interest like everybody else's mom?

I take the tickets from Breanna and force my smile wider. "Yeah, I guess so."

"Well, I can't wait to meet him."

Is everyone in the Hall of Champions staring at me? It feels like it. It's like someone turned a blinding spotlight on me and I forgot my lines. I shove the tickets in my purse and nod. "It's going to be exciting."

"I bet," Mom says. She starts to hand the clipboard back to Milo, but her expression changes. There's a darkness in the furrow of her brows. She clutches the sign-up sheet a little harder and reads aloud the line just before mine. "Emma Nolan and Anna Kendrickson?"

Please, please, floor, just open up and swallow me right now.

I pluck the clipboard from her hands and try to return it. "Sounds about right!"

"Two girls?" Mom lifts her chin. "The rules are very clear: no stag dates. There are too many people who want to come to prom and not enough tickets to go around. Couples only!"

"Oh, that *is* a couple, Mrs. Greene," Breanna helpfully supplies. She doesn't sound the slightest bit mean as she informs Mom, "Emma Nolan's gay."

Ice crackles around my mother. "Excuse me?"

Milo has perhaps spent a little too much time breathing the fumes in the cattle barn. He can't tell that my mother is about to get full dragon queen up in here; he thinks he's just clearing up some lingering confusion. "Yeah, she came out freshman year."

My mother lands just shy of mocking Milo's tone. "How lovely for her." She starts flipping through each page, her eyes sharp and scouring. When she gets back to the front, she informs Milo and Breanna, "You're done selling tickets for the day. Move along."

They look baffled, but this isn't their first rodeo with my mom. They zip their lips, lock the cashbox, and disappear.

An abyss swirls around me. It gets wider and deeper. The dark presses in from every side. I try to smile and lighten the moment and make this right. I'm desperate to make this right. "There's still another half an hour left of lunch, Mom. You can't close up shop early."

"Oh, I can, and I am," she says adamantly. She stares at the list again, disgust curling the arch of her lips. "I don't know who this Emma thinks she is, but we have standards here. We have morals."

"It's just a dance, Mom. It's fine."

Summoning up her full height, my mother glares at me. "It is *not* fine, Alyssa. Nothing about this is fine! I don't think so, and neither will the rest of the PTA, I guarantee you that."

"Why are you making a big deal out of this?" I ask. I already know what she's going to say. I already know because I've imagined variations on this conversation for three whole years. No matter how I approach it, I could never make this, make *queer*, okay for my mental mother. And god, now that it's happening for real, it's like I'm being torn in pieces. "It's one couple!"

"It's the principle of the matter!" Nostrils flaring, she looks away, some switch going off in her head. She points toward the office, thinking out loud. "I need to go have a word with Principal Hawkins."

Catching her by the hand, I say, "Mom, please!"

A thread of suspicion wraps around her. "You seem awfully invested in this, Alyssa."

Here, I could confess: *Because she's my girlfriend!* I could say, *Because she's my date. Because she loves me and I love her. Because there's nothing wrong with that. In fact, there's everything right with it!* But I can see my mother's fury and her fear. She grows with it, until she looks ten feet tall. She towers and glowers, all that stone wrapped around a heart of vulnerable flesh.

I guess I'm a coward. Instead of making any of the arguments I could make, I say, "I'm not."

For a moment, I think Mom sees through me. It's in the

way she tilts her head to the side, in the angle of her gaze as it sweeps across my face. It's like a strobe light goes off, and everything's illuminated for her. Then the dark comes again, and she pats me on the cheek. "Good girl. Let me worry about this."

I really am the worst person in the world, because I say nothing as she walks away.

5. Pitchforks Strongly Encouraged

EMMA

Thanks to Mrs. Greene, it's Emma season at school.

Of course she talked to Principal Hawkins. I don't know what he told her, but Mrs. Greene then called an *emergency* meeting of the PTA.

Never in the history of education has there been a PTA emergency. Like, omg, we don't have enough crepe paper for Spirit Week, we have to hit the Walmart like the fist of an angry god and correct that *immediately*!

Apparently, they also have to correct my existence.

The day after I volunteered as tribute—I mean, the day after I bought prom tickets for me and a celebrity that I'm definitely not asking to prom on the internet in the vain hope she'll actually show—the PTA sent an email to all the parents and students. It read:

> Dear James Madison Family,
>
> As you know, the PTA and the Future Corn Keepers of America host the annual prom

for our school. Excitement builds all year long for this event, and it's a highlight for our graduating seniors. We feel the need to remind everyone that attendance at prom is a privilege, not a right. As there have been questions, we want to clarify the requirements students must meet to attend:

GPA of 2.5 or above.[1]

Gentlemen are expected to wear a suit and tie.

Ladies are expected to wear modest evening attire, with dresses no shorter than knee length, no strapless gowns, no gowns that show belly or feature slits in the skirts to reveal skin above the knee, no material that is see-through or transparent, no material that is designed to appear see-through or transparent, no unusual materials (i.e., no duct tape dresses), and nothing that is designed to be sexually provocative, which will be determined at the discretion of the chaperones.[2]

Tickets will only be sold to boy/girl couples.[3] Due to space constraints, there will be no individual tickets sold, and no tickets sold to friends of the same sex. We want to make sure that everyone who has earned the right to attend this event with their date has the chance to.

Because prom tickets are limited, and because prom is meant to be a reward for our students at James Madison, only enrolled, eligible James Madison students[4] will be permitted to attend. No outside dates.

Thanks for your time, and we look forward to having a great prom this year!

> Sincerely,
> Your PTA
> Go Golden Weevils!

So, uh, that letter, wow. Let me tell you, I tore it apart on YouTube, point by point, starting at [1], that GPA requirement.

You know why it's that low? Because otherwise, half the basketball team would be barred from the prom. And that, of course, can never happen, because it would literally signal the Hoosier apocalypse. I've heard teachers aren't allowed to let the players' grades dip below that average, period. How lucky for them.

Moving on to [2], way to enshrine the patriarchy and gender binary. Only guys can show up in any old jacket and tie, but woOooOoo, beware the specter of a girl (and only a girl!) in a dress that shows her knees. Can you believe this one? You should, because that's the "classy, formal" version of the school's regular dress code. Guys who were assigned male at birth? Show up in some clothes, thanks. AFAB ladies, let me unfurl the scroll of respectability and modesty. Other genders? You don't exist.

Don't you love [3] and [4]? Those rules are brand-new. And they are stunning in their elegance. I'm almost proud of the bigots in our PTA, who CYAed twice without even once saying no gays allowed! It's almost like they know what they're doing is wrong! I mean, built-in plausible deniability, Golden Weevils PTA, well done! I would applaud them, but I can't. I'm too busy protecting myself from their demon seeds at school.

See, their kids tortured me all through freshman year and most of sophomore year but kind of got over the everyday offensive until just recently.

Recently, as in the minute this PTA letter was sent out and I got a bunch of online comments on my takedown. It's my channel, so most of the comments were on my side, you know? Can't have that!

Also, since Nan informed the school that I would be attending prom with anyone I wanted to, and if somebody had a problem with that, she had the ACLU on speed dial (whatever that is).

To be fair, she did ask me first. She only fights the fights I want her to—after I begged her not to go to the principal about the everyday awful stuff that happens because I knew it would make it ten times worse. But she gave my parents an epic talking-to, and when it made no difference, she cut them off like skin tags. While I cried in her arms, she promised to always be there if I needed her.

So after the email from the PTA, she held my chin in my hands and looked into my eyes. She asked, "Is this something you want, baby girl? You know it's going to be hard."

Maybe I hesitated, but not for long. My YouTube peeps are on my side, and that helps. And you know what? What I want doesn't hurt anybody. I've put up with their abuse since ninth grade, and I'm tired of it. I want to say goodbye to senior year with my date, at prom, like everybody else.

With tears in my eyes, and some caught in my throat, I told her, "I just want to dance with her, Nan."

She bobbed her head sharply. "Then we're doing this."

And she marched into school with me this past Monday morning. Swept me into the front office and demanded to speak to the principal. Said she'd sit on the counter until he was available, because, well, Nan has a way of making a point when she wants to.

Principal Hawkins, I need to tell you, is really nice. First, he listened. He covered Nan's white hands with his brown ones and listened to every single word she said without interrupting.

Then, when she was finished, he turned to me and said, "Prom isn't sponsored by the school. It doesn't come out of our budget, we don't plan it. We allow the committee to throw it here for free."

"But the money goes to a school club," I said. "It's run by the PTA."

"And I'll point that out in the meeting, Emma. You just have to understand that I only have so much power over this. If it escalates, I'll go as far as I can. You just have to know that I can't stop this all by myself."

It didn't seem right or fair that the principal couldn't make the rules about our school prom. But there it was. To be honest, I thought I should cry, but all I felt was numb. Nan reached over and stroked my back; it was like a ghost of a touch.

Principal Hawkins waited a moment, then said, "I can warn them that their prom includes you, or they need to find another site. Hopefully, that will turn things around. Money's pretty tight all over since the plant closed down."

"Okay."

"There's still a chance it could make things worse. This is a big deal, Emma. Are you sure you want me to go forward?"

Was I? I was. And yet, even though I got a rush of adrenaline, somehow, I couldn't get enough breath to say yes. So I nodded instead. The deal was sealed. He promised to talk to the PTA, and I know he kept his word.

How? Well, the PTA did *not* send out a new email. Instead, they whispered a rumor and made sure it spread like sparks in the night: if Emma Nolan insists on queering up this year's prom, then prom is gonna be canceled. They can't afford to host it anywhere else; this is all my fault.

And you know, we don't have a lot going on in Edgewater. I think you can probably tell. Sometimes a tent revival will come to town, and that's exciting because people fall down and speak in tongues.

There's fair season, when everybody's competing with prize calves and wedding ring quilts.

And let's not forget the wonder and glory of cruising the Walmart parking lot on Saturday night. (Yes, we have a movie theater, but it shows one movie at a time, and usually something super old.)

Friends, Golden Weevils basketball games, and prom? Those are *the* social highlights of our limited calendar. And now everybody thinks one of them's about to get canceled because of *me*.

And that means all the abuse from freshman year is happening again, only this time, with purpose. The chanting is back—annoying but ignorable. There are worse things people could whisper at me, but I have to say, "Gay, gay, gay" offends on an artistic level.

It lacks creativity. There's a whole internet out there for people who can't think for themselves; it's literally a gateway to thousands of slurs with bite, with real shape to them. Instead, these doofuses pick the dictionary definition of me and croak it like a choir of narrow-minded frogs.

Oh, and bow down, because I'm now the Moses of southern Indiana. Wherever I go, seas part for me to pass. Hall of Champions, English class, cafeteria, doesn't matter: students who had forgotten they cared I was gay suddenly recoil again. I am my own personal cootie factory, open for business for the first time since *kindergarten*.

Oh, and this morning, I had to relearn the importance of keeping *nothing* important in my locker. See, during freshman year, people squeezed packets of Zesty French dressing from the cafeteria through the vents and ruined my favorite jacket.

To this day, I tense up when I smell sweetness and vinegar.

I started using the locker again when things tapered in junior year. I didn't store anything super important in it, but guess what?

Today, the very clever students of James Madison High found a way to squirt lotion through the vents. When I opened it after lunch, I found everything coated in a thick, pearly layer of Jergens. Including a history textbook that leaves out the reason for the Civil War.

I took it to the office to get a new one, and the secretary (whose desk Nan threatened to sit on) told me *I* have to pay to replace it. She didn't care why it was ruined or who had a hand in it. My book, my responsibility. That'll be eighty dollars, please.

My nan doesn't have that kind of money just lying around, so I'll have to cash out my Patreon savings. So much for a new guitar this year.

Through all of this, normally, I'd lean on my girlfriend for support. But outside of school, I haven't seen Alyssa in almost two weeks.

Once her mother started leading this particular mob of angry townsfolk, she ended up on lockdown. We text at night, stolen moments during econ homework, quick Snaps so there's no evidence left behind. And, you know, I know why she's hiding. Most of me is glad she's safe in her invisibility.

I just wish I didn't have to be visible all alone.

Principal Hawkins says he's doing everything he can behind the scenes, Alyssa is heartbroken behind our screens, but that leaves me by myself, in front of *them*.

I make myself go to school. I make myself show up for each class. Every day, each step is heavier as the clock ticks toward three, then I burst out of my seat the second the last bell rings.

Seniors get to leave their classes first. We have a whole twenty-minute passing period—mostly so people who drive can get out of the parking lot before the buses leave. Car riders wait at the front doors, and this week, Nan's been picking me up because . . . well, her *forty*-year-old car seems safer than a fairly new bus full of enemies and no way out.

Today's only different because it's raining, and I have to wait inside. Arms wrapped around myself, I stare out the front doors while I watch for Nan's blue VW Beetle. I have my Moses circle around me, isolating but safe, right? Then I hear something behind me. A weird shuffling, a concentrated rustle.

Pushing up my glasses, I look back.

Everyone's eyes are turned away from me. I know all of these faces; they're not even the most popular kids at school. They're medium-ordinary. They just think they're better than me because they're straight.

They talk at each other so hard, it looks like their jaws might fly off. It's not natural, but they're not *doing* anything. I try to warn with a dark expression, but I'm afraid it comes out plaintive instead.

I turn back to the doors. My breath steams the glass as I lean on the metal frame. There's no point in texting. Nan always puts her phone in the glove box. Therefore, I try telepathy. *Nan, come on, please hurry.*

Then it happens.

Something hard bounces off the back of my head and falls

to the floor. Instinctively, I throw a hand up, but there's no cut. No blood. Probably not even a bruise. It takes me a second, but I find the projectile wobbling to a stop on the floor.

A quarter.

Like, somebody has enough pocket change that they skipped the pennies and nickels and dimes and went straight for a quarter. Once again, I cast a look at the people around me. Once again, they're coincidentally all craning in other directions. It doesn't keep them from laughing, though. Little, trapped snickers escape them.

Even as my insides turn to sick, green goo, I lean over and snatch up the coin. With a wave, I make a show of shoving it into my pocket. "Thanks. Now I have enough money to take your mom on a date."

Then I punch through the doors and into the rain.

6. Camouflage

ALYSSA

Shelby Kinnunen opens the door for me, and I back into the gym with a giant box of cardboard.

It's reclaimed, from the recycling program the student council started this year in the cafeteria. Even though it smells like corn dog nuggets, it's free, and it's plentiful. Hefting the box a little higher, I say, "We're going to make so many stars with this."

"Don't know why we're bothering," Shelby says, twirling off the door and following me inside. There are people at work as far as the eye can see. The president and vice president of every single club at school have shown up to work on prom decorations. It's tradition; it really makes the dance our own.

"We're making it nice," I reply. "It's more special this way, isn't it?"

Shelby rolls her shoulders lazily. She's here as the cheer captain, but I feel like we're friends. I mean, I feel like everyone here is at least friend*ly*. It's not a big school, or a big town, so we all have a lot in common.

When I move to put my box of boxes down, Shelby leans in to help and whispers to me, "I heard it's getting canceled."

An icy drop of panic falls on my heart. I've heard that, too—from my mother. Not directly, but she's not exactly quiet on the phone these days. Her voice falls to a murmur, but I hear her campaigning with the other parents. They workshopped the new PTA prom rules together and celebrated when they sent them out.

Somehow, they didn't see it coming, that Emma's grandmother would fire back. I could have told Mom. I've been secretly having dinner with Emma and Nan Nolan for three years now. When Nan decides to do something, she goes all in. She painted her house purple, I'm not even kidding. Actual, grapey, Jolly Rancher purple—with lime green trim.

So if my mother had thought about it for even a second, she would have realized that bringing in the ACLU wasn't just a threat—even though that's exactly what it felt like. Oh yes. And then it made her even madder when Principal Hawkins said he *agreed* with Nan. Oh my gosh, Mom went from annoyed to red-flag-in-a-bullfighting-ring mad, baseball-bat-against-a-hornet's-nest kind of mad.

Since then, she's been gauging support for a cancellation, and I think that's my fault.

I pointed out to her that if we can't take outside dates, that means I can't go with John Cho. (Let's set aside the fact that he's famous, grown up, and has no idea I exist.) Theoretically, Mom's rule meant no perfect, perfect prom for me either.

With a wave of her hand, she said, "Oh, Alyssa, you know that doesn't apply to you."

"Uh no," I told her. I actually stamped my foot, and felt ridiculous when I did it. "The rules are the rules. They apply to me or they don't apply to anyone."

Mom walked away from me. And then the whispering started. The phone calls and frantic messages. Her fingers flew so fast, the chime of incoming texts sounded like an arcade. She talked to the PTA and everybody's parents at our church, who, of course, told their kids, and that's how rumors get started.

The one thing that keeps me from completely losing it is that everybody's feelings are mixed when it comes to calling off the prom. It's the usual *seniors won't get their senior year back; not fair to punish everybody because one person wants to break the rules* kind of stuff. For once, entropy is on the side of good.

So I feel comfortable telling Shelby, "That's not going to happen. Prom is for everybody, and everybody looks forward to it."

Twisting the dark coils of her hair into a loose braid, Shelby shrugs again. "I get that. You get that. Why doesn't she? Is it really going to kill her to stay home and *not* shave her legs that night?"

Fire blazes in my stomach. She knows *nothing* about Emma. She doesn't have the first inkling. There are so many beautiful things in Emma Nolan that we're lucky to have her in Edgewater at all. Her heart is so big when she doesn't have to protect it.

I mean, she feeds the squirrels on purpose—she feels bad for them, because everybody else tries to keep them out of their yards. When Emma turns her attention on you, it will break your heart because you've never been so *seen* in your life.

All these little people, with all their little minds, constantly spitting on her—for no reason. Because their pastors say so, because their parents say so. Not because they care, or think, or decide for themselves. And I want to say all of that, but instead, I sit on the polished wood floor and reach for the scissors. "That's really mean."

"I'm joking," Shelby says, not joking at all. "But I'm super sad, Alyssa! Kevin was *supposed* to prompose to me, like, the day after Nick did Kaylee. But they quit selling the tickets, and now he, like . . . wants to wait and see what happens. It's like I'm personally being punished."

My whole life, I've been lucky that when I get mad, I don't get hot in the face. The tips of my ears, yes. And across my chest, definitely. But I don't *look* angry. The sound of it doesn't come out in my voice. That makes it easier to try to talk sense to people who have completely lost the plot. "Well, she's being punished, too."

Shelby stops, the glue she's pouring into her paper plate still dripping. "How?"

Calmly, I repeat, "Prom is for everybody. Emma included."

With disgust, Shelby puts the glue down and starts stirring it around with a broken piece of leftover cardboard. We're going to slop that onto the stars I'm getting ready to cut out of nugget boxes and then dip them in the glitter tray. At least, we are if we can get through this conversation and back to work. "There are rules."

"Rules the PTA *just* invented."

"No, they were just unspoken rules before."

I sigh and catch Shelby's gaze. "Did you care if Emma went to the prom *before* she signed up?"

Oh. Oh, there it is. A tiny flicker of self-awareness; of course she didn't. Before Emma signed up, all Shelby, and Kaylee, and everybody else cared about was getting *their* promposal and getting *their* special night. But instead of admitting that, Shelby stares me down. "I'm kind of wondering why you care so much *after*."

Danger! Warning! The heat spreads across my chest and down into my belly. Is she clocking me? Shelby's never struck me as all that observant, but maybe it was an act. Can she look into me and see that I'm not *just* arguing for Emma? That I want this night for me, too?

I cannot let that rumor start. Not now. My mother has to find out from me, at the right time, in the right way. Hands shaking, I put down the scissors. "I'm the president of student council. I work for every student, not just the popular ones."

Out of nowhere, Shelby's boyfriend, Kevin McCalla, slides on his knees and right into our pile of cardboard. At the last second, he ditches onto his back, like he's crashing into a pile of autumn leaves.

He thinks this is charming; you can tell by the way he cheese-grins at Shelby when he comes to a stop. He's practically in her lap. That's probably against some unspoken rules, too, and yet, there he is. "Why so serious, babes?"

"Just talking about Emma," Shelby replies.

"You mean Ho-meo and Juliet?"

My temper slips; I slap a hand down on the cardboard by

Kevin's head. Stray flecks of glitter leap up like fleas. "We have a no-tolerance bullying policy in this school!"

He laughs, baffled. "I didn't say it to *her*."

"That's not the point."

Shelby looks me over again. "Again, you're getting very LGBTOMG over this, Alyssa. Something you want to share?"

"You know what I want to share?" I ask, pulling it all back in. Swallowing it all down. It's ridiculous, but I literally feel like Elsa in *Frozen*, and how sad is it that a cartoon is the only thing I can think of to calm myself down? I can't *feel* this right now. I can't let it show. Kevin and Shelby aren't exactly bloodhounds, but if I lose my temper . . .

Talking with my hands, I say, "I want to share my prom night with anybody who wants to be there. Because I don't want anybody to stand in the way of me and the dance that I have been thinking about since I was twelve. I already have my dress. I already have my tickets. I want to have this. And I want you to have it, too. I want us *all* to have it. Is that so wrong?"

I don't think Shelby or Kevin feels bad at all, but they both shrug. She says, "Whatever."

He says, "Whatever, who cares?"

Twin whatevers in the face of something so monumental, and they can't even see it. I'm glad they don't see it.

Yes, I hate myself for hiding it. But I'm doing what I can— as much as I can—to help this blow over. With all of the push-back Mom's getting over canceling, I really feel like the PTA is close to deciding it's not worth the fight. If the Shelbys and Kaylees and Kevins and Nicks of James Madison High decide they want their prom more than they want to keep Emma away, that *helps*.

They'll put pressure on their parents; Principal Hawkins will push back from the school. If we can just ride this out, just a couple days more, I really believe my mother and the rest of the PTA will give up on this. They just need to be able to step back quietly, without losing face.

And the sooner that happens, the sooner I can sit my mother down and talk some sense into her. Or at least talk some understanding into her. I promised Emma that we'd go to prom together, and I meant it.

I can't be—I *won't* be—one more person in her life who loves her then lets her down.

7. Enter Stage Left

EMMA

One more day out on my own, ducking my head and making myself as small as possible as I move between classes at school.

Alyssa thinks the rumors are dying down. I think she's wearing the thickest, rosiest glasses in history. It's easy for her to think it's getting better. She's basically in the next county, watching the tornado snake along in the distance. I'm the spinning cow, whirling around inside it.

My back aches under the weight of my bag. Now that I can't use my locker at all, I'm carrying around fifteen thousand pounds of textbooks, a conservative estimate. The diesel-sniffing mob around me doesn't know that, though.

So as I turn down the hall toward my locker, I feel eyes on me. It must be a Spidey sense at this point. I know when they're lurking, watching, waiting.

If they want to keep throwing quarters, I'm good with that. But no, apparently somebody taught them the value of money because that's not what awaits me this time. People edge back from me; I take each step warily.

"Gaybo," someone mutters.

Another whispers, "Lezzie."

The insults sink into my skin, tangling into a black knot that permanently lives in the pit of my stomach. I thought I was over caring what people say about me, but I guess not. The sad thing is, I don't even want people to like me anymore. I just wish they'd leave me alone. I have a feeling that I would be very forgettable if I lived anywhere else.

When I steal a look up, I see two red balloons bobbing above our heads. I don't have to get closer to know they're the *X* that marks the spot. But oh, what treasures await me?

During Spirit Week, the cheerleaders decorate all the jocks' lockers. It's not unusual to see signs, balloons, ribbons, tiny awnings and faux gems, silk curtains and streamers. They've got this down to a science, with their perfect stick-and-bead hand-lettering and their eye for accessories. I'm sure all of these skills will come in useful later in life.

But let's be real, y'all. There's just one locker decorated right now, and this may come as a surprise to you, but I'm not athletic at all.

Voices drop; the hallway goes eerily quiet. Is this an improvement over the constant chatter of people three centuries shy of whispering *burn the witch* at me? I don't know. What I do know is that whatever's on my locker, I'm going to ignore it. They don't get the satisfaction of a reaction.

I lift my chin but look down and forward. I'm probably all Hunchback of Notre Dame right now, but so? Just breathe, Emma. Just walk, one foot in front of the other.

I try to summon the picture of golden, sandy beaches, or even just the grayish-beige shores of Indiana Beach.

Think about holding Alyssa's hand at Holiday World. It's small and soft; she feels delicate next to me. She'd want me to smile and nod; I don't think I can. Namaste and pray to get the hell away from here, that's the best I can do. There's a Greyhound ticket in my future. I don't even care where it goes. Focus on that. On freedom and escape and—

Yes. Good. Breathe. I'm breathing, and I'm not listening, and I'm not looking—not, not looking except I just caught a glimpse. Now I can't tear my eyes away.

This time, it's not lotion or dressing. It's not even graffiti for the custodians to scrub clean. No, it's two red balloons to mark the hanging of a rainbow teddy bear. Somebody took the time to make a *noose*. They took the time to string it through the locker vents, so a pride-flavored Beanie Boo could bite the dust.

I can't breathe through this. I reach out and yank the noose free. I feel small and sharp and brittle, cutting looks at the people around me. They hold back like a wave. They want to crash over me, but they don't dare. They're cowards, every single one of them.

"Nice," I say, waving the Beanie Boo at them. "Real nice."

Breaking free from the crowd, Kaylee washes up against me. With a sickly sweet smile, she asks, "Do you like it? We got it just for you."

"Yeah, you know what? I'm pretty sure this is one step past breaking school rules, Kaylee. This is a death threat."

Kaylee's eyes widen with disingenuous sincerity. "It's our way of saying thank you, Emma!"

Now that Kaylee broke the seal and spoke to me, her centurion Shelby steps up and adds, "Yeah! Thanks for canceling prom!"

When I wave my shaking hands, I feel myself lose balance. My backpack is too heavy, my heart is too broken, my brain is too fried. My voice cracks when I say, "Prom isn't canceled!"

Just then, Alyssa appears. At once, it's like the sun rises, and hope fills my heart. She's trying to save me, even though she has a secret. Even though she risks exposure when she takes my side. Her gaze slides past mine, but she steps between me and Kaylee. "That's enough. Leave her alone."

"We're just talking," Kaylee says. She looks around Alyssa, threatening me with a smile. "Right, Emma?"

I don't say anything. I refuse to degrade myself. I refuse to be complicit. But it's like my presence answers for me. Just by standing there, I'm making them angry. Just by breathing, I make it worse. I want to grab Alyssa and run away with her, far away from here, somewhere we can just be. Instead, I stand stock-still and try not to cry.

"Walk away," Alyssa says, gathering the full mantle of the student council presidency around her.

"Oh, is that how it is?" Cocking her head to one side, Kaylee sounds the slightest bit hurt. That dissipates instantly, converted into pure primary school bile. "So you're on her side."

"No," Alyssa says, a shot right through my heart. "I'm just not in third grade."

A muffled roar laps the hallway. Someone is two seconds from yelling, "Fight, fight!" Then Nick and Kevin melt out of the mob like twin grease stains. They back up their girlfriends in a way that I, if I were their girlfriends, would dump them for on the spot.

Nick says, "Kaylee. Babe. It's okay. She can bring her queer-bait girlfriend to the prom if she lets us watch."

With a leer, Kevin nods. "Add some memories to the spank bank."

Suddenly, a voice booms out. My knees go out from under me in relief. Principal Hawkins stalks down the hallway. Students peel away and disappear as fast as they can. Recreational felonies are only fun if you don't get caught.

"Gentlemen," Principal Hawkins says, then, "Ladies. I don't know what's going on here, but it's over."

Kaylee shrugs and goes to walk away. She makes a wide circle around Alyssa, just so she can "accidentally" bump my shoulder. With a purposeful whisper at my side, she says, "Oh, Emma. Unlike your social life, this is *not* over."

Whither goest Kaylee, so goes her ragtag nation of troglodytes who are going to peak in high school. Shelby vines herself around Kevin, and Nick throws an arm over Kaylee's shoulder. When they finally drift around the corner, I exhale and collapse. Though I know they're on my side, it's hard to face Alyssa and Principal Hawkins.

"I'm sorry," I say, even though it's not my fault. I hold up the bear helplessly.

Principal Hawkins eyes it in my hand. His kind face hardens, and he straightens his back. "This is unacceptable, Emma. We'll find out who did it, and they'll be handled appropriately."

"Please don't," I say. "Things are bad enough as it is."

Alyssa puts a hand on my arm. Her dark eyes are liquid,

too. I feel the pull between us; it's hard not to give in. If I could collapse in her arms, everything—well, it wouldn't be all right. But it would be better, at least for a moment. Softly, she says, "If you let them get away with it . . ."

"No, it's not worth it." Folding into myself again, I can barely say it above a whisper, but I do say it: "Maybe none of this is worth it."

Principal Hawkins shakes his head. "No, uh-uh. You have rights, Emma. I have an email from the ACLU liaison. They're prepared to step in if they have to. In fact, they said your case has already attracted some attention online."

"Besides on my channel?" I say, stunned.

"Oh yes. This is a big deal," Principal Hawkins says. "For you, absolutely. But for all the kids just like you, too."

I blink in disbelief. "What are you saying? I'm like a gay, white Rosa Parks?"

Principal Hawkins gives me *a look.* "Uh, no. I'm absolutely not saying that."

"You're the gay, white Emma Nolan," Alyssa says. "You're leading *this* charge."

"Exactly. And I'm proud to be a part of that," Principal Hawkins says. "This is so much better than dealing with students on meth."

At that, Alyssa and I both rear our heads back and say, "Wut?"

Principal Hawkins waves it off. "I've got a principal friend in Terre Haute. All he deals with are bad smells and meth, all day long."

For some reason, that breaks the heaviness of the moment.

I laugh in spite of myself. No, not myself. In spite of everyone else. I laugh because I'm not on drugs. I laugh because the legal cavalry is coming. I laugh because . . . because I need it. I even slump against Alyssa. Just a little bit, just for a moment.

"Well, I'm not on meth yet. We'll see how the next couple of days go."

"We'll get you through this," Principal Hawkins promises.

And then Milo Potts, the FCK treasurer, comes screaming around the corner. Both figuratively—he's running at top speed—and literally, his voice cracking. "Principal Hawkins! Principal Hawkins! Come quick!"

Calmly, Principal Hawkins approaches him. "Everything's going to be all right, Milo. What's going on?"

"There are people outside," Milo shouts. "They have picket signs about prom!"

Oh. Crap.

8. The Invasion

ALYSSA

There is trouble right here in Edgewater, Indiana. Crammed behind three sets of double doors that lead into the parking lot, I stand with Emma as we stare at the picketers outside.

We're not the only ones. It feels like most of the high school is pressed in here with us. The small space buzzes like a beehive, and it's unbearably hot with so many bodies and so little room. Also, it smells like at least half the people in here just finished gym class without hitting the showers. But we have to be pressed to the glass, because we can't miss the biggest show ever to hit James Madison High.

Outside, Principal Hawkins stands on the curb, his back to us. He's got one hand on his hip, and the other—I'm guessing—clapped to his brow. Though we're all dying to hear what's going on out there, Principal Hawkins told us to stay inside, and he said it in a Stern Dad voice that would make most of us feel legitimately guilty for letting him down. It feels like there are hundreds of cell phones flashing, all turned toward the parking lot . . . and the strangers with protest signs that fill it.

"Who are these people?" I ask under my breath.

Emma subtly loops her pinkie with mine and squeezes. "I don't know."

Nearby, somebody reads one of the signs as it turns toward us. "Classically trained singer dancer activist?"

"What the hell?" somebody else says.

I'm speechless. Literally. A dark-haired woman carries a sign that reads ANNIE GET YOUR GIRL, and the sign is the least striking thing about her. Her hair is short and tight, and her lipstick is one shade darker than blood-red. She's wearing this jumpsuit-pantsuit thing in the same scarlet, and her heels are sharp enough to serve steak-on-a-stick at the county fair. When she stops to talk to Principal Hawkins, she talks with her whole body: shoulders thrown back, hand gesturing at the sky.

Whatever she's saying, Principal Hawkins hangs on every word. He's a moth caught in her light, nodding and nodding and nodding.

From behind us, Nick and Kevin boom out, "Go! Go! GooooolDEN?!"

Everyone else calls back, "WEEEEvils, go, go!"

With that display of athletic privilege, Nick and Kevin cut through the crowd. Arms held out straight, they shove open the front doors. And since they're the most popular guys in school, everybody else pours out behind them.

In the rush, I lose hold of Emma's pinkie and we're swept out of different doors. I can't even hope to get back to her until everybody stops pushing.

"Hey," a guy yells, "it's Mr. Pecker!"

And ... he's right! My mouth drops open, and I stare at the heavyset man with the NO MORE MR. NICE GAY sign.

He's probably Principal Hawkins's age, but he has a perfectly smooth face that's instantly recognizable. He used to play the weird neighbor on *Talk to the Hand*, which we all watched in middle school.

He was so popular, they even aired extra webisodes with him. They're probably still online, in fact. Whenever the kids on the show got into some kind of trouble, he'd randomly burst in and try to solve everything. Usually in ways that blew up in his face and threatened to destroy property.

And now he's at James Madison High, in a silver-gray suit, carrying a blatantly pro-LGBTQ sign. When people recognize him—and you can tell they do, because suddenly there's an echo of "Pecker, Pecker, Pecker!" in the air—he throws his head back ever so slightly. Like he's soaking their attention up, like it has a reverse-aging effect. His skin *is* really smooth—maybe it does.

"All students," Principal Hawkins booms, his voice rising over the crowd, "need to return to their homeroom classes immediately!"

"Why?" booms the brunette woman. Impressively, her voice carries better than our principal's does. She's shorter than he is but somehow takes up all of the space in their tight little circle. "Are you afraid of a little truth? Are you afraid these young Indianans will be exposed to ... the truth?!"

Principal Hawkins raises his hands. "No, this is a matter of safet—"

The woman cuts him off. "Sir, I am *the* Dee Dee Allen, and

the spotlight only dims when I will it! I read three-quarters of a news story about dear little Emma Nolan, and I knew I had to come!"

I turn my head so fast, I think I pop something in my spine. Across the way, Emma freezes. I recognize that look on her face, the flight-because-she's-not-going-to-fight face. Suddenly, everyone's looking at her. It couldn't have been scripted more perfectly. Emma's face is bright red, and she clutches the strangled teddy bear in her hands.

"This," Dee Dee Allen, mysterious picketer, continues, "is an OUTRAGE! You act like a mob of angry villagers while poor Emma's heart breaks! And let me tell you, I've played Mrs. Potts in *Beauty and the Beast*; I know all about angry mobs!"

"Ms. Allen," Principal Hawkins says, but she interrupts him.

"The prom should be for everyone! Straight and gay and LGBTQIA! Plus all the other letters I don't know, but are all equally worthy of love!"

Now the kids around me start to roil and boil, a kettle full of indignation. People shout back, but it's a mush of sound. The kind of mush that signals the beginning of a riot, actually.

Little spikes of panic race through me. I don't think anything really bad will happen, but this . . . this feels like something really bad might happen. I look to Emma again. Her face is strained and anxious. I know she feels the turn in the crowd, too. And she knows—*we* know—that if they turn, it'll be on her.

I am the student council president. I have a responsibility.

The last thing I want is for everyone to stare at me and speculate about me. But actually, the last thing I want is for everybody here to hurt Emma. They already threatened her today; this could be the spark before the bang.

Without another thought, I act. Jumping up on the concrete benches, I throw my hands out. As loud as I can, I call out, "Go! Go! GooooolDEN?!"

And like it's built into their DNA, my fellow students all turn toward me and bellow back, "WEEEEvils, go, go!"

Now that I have all the attention, Ms. Allen and—I hate to call him Mr. Pecker, but I don't know what else to say—Mr. Pecker look incredibly annoyed. I don't care. They're not my concern. My classmates are.

With everyone looking to me expectantly, I try not to let the woozy feeling in my chest spread too far. Fainting would probably put an end to this dangerous situation, but taking a header into cement seems like it would be counterintuitive.

Rubbing my hands on my jeans, I say, "These fine people, whoever they are, have a right to their opinion. And . . . and so do you. Everybody should be heard. People have been whispering about prom for too long now. As your student council president, I am saying here and now, let's have that talk. I'm officially inviting everyone to a public meeting in the gym tonight at six thirty to hash this out, once and for all."

I'm absolutely sure I hear Ms. Allen mutter, "Who is this broad?" but I don't care. Emma catches my eye, then jerks a thumb over her shoulder. She's not dumb—she's getting out of here before she gets hurt. Since all eyes are on the parking lot,

Emma slips back into the school and disappears from sight. I don't know if she's going to bail on the rest of the day or what, and I don't need to. Wherever she's going, she's safe, and that's what matters.

My mouth is instantly dry, but I wave a hand at our picketers. "Ms. Allen, Mr. . . . ." I don't want to say *Pecker*.

Graciously, the man waves a hand in a flourish and projects, "Glickman. Barry Glickman, star of stage and screen!"

"Thank you, Mr. Glickman. You and Ms. Allen are welcome to come tonight." I turn to the students, who stare at me, and I can't even make out their expressions. Their faces are rapt but unfocused. I hold out my arms to them. "And you're all invited. So are your parents. Everybody gets a say. This is our school. We *will* protect it. But this is also our community, and we *will* respect it. All of it."

Now that the spell is broken, Principal Hawkins puts a hand on Ms. Allen's arm—a really kind of familiar hand, if you ask me. But he regains his authority, and the sharp look that makes even the most beef-hearted senior quail.

"Thank you, Miss Greene! Now that we've set a time to discuss the issue, this gathering is over. Everyone, and I mean everyone, needs to return to their classes immediately."

"But, Tom," Ms. Allen says, intoning his first name like they're long-lost friends, distress written across her face in broad strokes. "We haven't even met the girl!"

"Later," Principal Hawkins tells her.

My classmates break and trickle back inside. Slowly, because you never know when something else might happen, but they keep moving. They straggle until there's no one left outside but me, Principal Hawkins, and a handful of strangers with picket signs.

Emma's gone. Long gone. And even though I put a stop to the human tsunami that threatened to drown her, guilt gnaws in my stomach. I could have done more. Or better. Or something. Because now that the blur of adrenaline is fading, suddenly the realization of what I've actually done settles in.

I just asked everybody in Edgewater to come testify at Emma's witch trial.

Oh no.

A little dizzy, I sink down to sit on the bench, rather than stepping down and staying on my feet. Principal Hawkins exchanges a few more quiet words with Ms. Allen and Mr. Glickman, then strides over to me.

Even though I've never been in trouble at any point during my four-year high school career, I crumple a little as he approaches. To my surprise, he sits down beside me and puts a hand on my shoulder. "You showed an incredible amount of leadership just now, Alyssa."

Weakly, I say, "Didn't I make it worse?"

"No," he says. His voice is warm and low and comforting. "I think you did what we should have done weeks ago. You've dragged this out of the shadows. You're insisting we handle this civilly and discuss the issue like human beings."

Glancing past him, I see Ms. Allen and Mr. Glickman in their own discussion huddle. To Principal Hawkins, and only to him, I admit, "*They* forced the issue. I was just trying to calm everyone down."

"And you don't think that was worthwhile?"

For a moment, I'm quiet. Finally, I shake my head, "No, I do."

"Don't let perfect be the enemy of good, Alyssa. Every step we make toward better is a step in the right direction."

At this moment, I can hear Emma cracking a joke about how Hallmark card that sounds. But also laughing at his sincerity—not in a cruel way, just in disbelief. In surprise that anyone can be that optimistic, that full of hope.

I don't think it's funny, though. Those words lodge into me, right between my ribs, the tip of their arrow just nicking my heart.

Don't let perfect be the enemy of good.

Not perfect. Just good.

Wow.

9. John Proctor Problems

EMMA

In general, going back to school after the school day is over is not high on my list of good times to be had.

And it still isn't. Nan and I pull up to the school at a quarter till six in the hope that I can find Alyssa and talk to her first. But there's no way that's happening, because a veritable river of people pour off a bus that says BROADWAY ACROSS THE STATES on the side of it. They have signs, they wear bright colors, they have hair lengths that are inappropriate for both the guys *and* the girls around these parts.

Streaming across the parking lot, they march toward the single illuminated door in the dark school: the one that leads to the gym. Their voices ring up to the night sky, singing snatches of show tunes I don't recognize and barking out cadences I do. They're here, they're queer, and they cordially invite the people of my high school to get over it.

They crash into the Extremely Angry Parents of James Madison High on the sidewalk, mingling like a violent smoothie that no one in their right mind would want to taste. They force a bottleneck at the doors, with people shot through them seemingly at random. The parents yell at the Broadway people to go home and, even *better*, to go back where they belong. Right in front of all the reporters, who round out the melee.

Parked along the curb, there are two news vans: one from Evansville, which isn't far from us, and one from Indianapolis, which is both far *and* our state capital. They have lights and video cameras, complementing the reporters with just camera-cameras who keep trying to fish people out of the stream to give statements.

Mr. Thu and Mr. Gonsalves, our school security guards, are doing what they can to keep everyone calm. The way they gently urge the horde inside results in a process about as graceful as stuffing a cattle chute. Which is to say: people move, but it ain't pretty.

Nan and I straggle back a little. She clutches my hand, sure and strong. "Bet they wish they'd just let you go to prom in peace, huh?"

"I'm starting to wish we'd just gone with boys and ditched them after we got there," I reply. That's only 15 percent true. Maybe 25. The number falls and rises with each step I take. Angry voices spill from the gym already. The meeting's not supposed to start for another half hour, but it's already bedlam when we get inside.

The bleachers on either side of the gym are pulled out, but hardly anyone is using them. The Broadway people wave their picket signs on one side, and the only local over there with them is our resident anarchist-slash-goth, who is basically on whatever side causes the most trouble. She ran a student council campaign on the slogan *End the Tyranny of Tater Tots at Lunch.* (She lost.)

The locals shake their spirit cowbells (ten dollars each, available at the bookstore or the box office at any Golden Weevils home game) angrily on the other side. They don't chant. They don't sing. But they do yell at the Broadway people, so loudly that the veins on their collective foreheads jut out in syncopated time.

I've never spent a lot of time picturing what sound looks like. Buuuut, I've just walked into Hieronymus Bosch's *Cacophony*, gouache on board, 2019.

My fingertips tingle. So do my toes. Something heavy keeps thumping into my ribs from the inside, then crashing against the inside of my skull. I could be having a heart attack. Or a stroke. Or both! That would probably make me a modern medical miracle, way more newsworthy than falling in love with a girl and wanting to go to prom.

Alyssa, my Alyssa, stands next to Principal Hawkins. Her dark hair falls in perfect cascades over her shoulders. She's wearing the same outfit she wore to Model UN, a gray jacket and pencil skirt, black patent heels. She looks so professional up there, so accomplished.

And yet, she holds a megaphone and stares at the mess her meeting has already become. There's despair in her eyes and discontent on her coral lips. When she texted me about it, she made it sound like a tea party. Everyone gathered to respectfully discuss whether or not I deserve civil rights. I mean, she didn't put it *that* way, but the emphasis was on how orderly it would be.

Well. This is super orderly, if you're into turf wars. On the left side, the Sharks with their picket signs. On the right, the Jets with their cowbells. No guns, no knives, but make no mistake, there will be absolutely no survivors.

Finally, Alyssa realizes one very important thing. She has the megaphone. She fiddles with the buttons, and suddenly, a loud siren fills the gym. The sound bounces off the concrete block walls and hardwood floor, and people will probably still hear it echoing in two hundred years.

But it does the job; people hush.

Alyssa raises the megaphone and speaks into it. "Thank you all for coming to this town hall meeting. My name is Alyssa Greene; I'm the student council president."

Mrs. Greene snatches the megaphone and squawks into it. "And I am Elena Greene, the president of the PTA! I'm here to represent the parents of this community. I have listened to their concerns and have taken them as my very own. Together, we established rules for this year's prom! Rules that affect everyone, not just Emma Nolan!"

Now, I've met Mrs. Greene. She's used to getting the very last word on everything. I cover my mouth to keep from laughing out loud when Dee Dee Allen reaches across the aisle and snatches the megaphone from her. "Oh, you established some *rules*, did you? I know what's going on here, and frankly, I'm appalled!"

It's horrifying in a very real and concrete way that everybody is in this gym because I want a date night with my girl. But it's also really gratifying to see somebody stand up to Mrs. Greene on my behalf.

Gently, Principal Hawkins takes the megaphone for himself. He waves calming hands, encouraging everybody to sit down. Nan and I sit near the very people protesting my entire existence, just because it seems like it would be weird to sit with strangers. But it's weird over here, too. Moses circle, still in effect. People slide away from me on the bleachers, creating a little island, population: Nan and me.

"Thank you all for coming," Principal Hawkins says. "Thank you all for your concern. And thank you to Alyssa Greene for stepping up and taking control of this situation. She's a remarkable young woman and the kind of leader that makes James Madison stronger. Everyone, Alyssa Greene."

Politely, people applaud. And you can tell it's just polite, because voices rumble and shrill in the stands. Each side is talking to itself. Everyone's just waiting for their turn to talk. My best guess is there will be no listening here tonight. But hey, my tiny Hoosier town that greeted daylight saving time like it was the work of the Devil is absolutely welcome to prove me wrong.

Alyssa thanks Principal Hawkins. Her hands shake—I see them from here. I wish I could catch them between mine and calm them. I wish I could whisper into her ear how great she's about to be. This moment is huge, not because she's out—but because she's *not*.

She's risking everything with her mother to speak up for me; she's risking exposing herself to everyone at school. Yes, I want people to know that we're in love, but right now, I just want them to appreciate how brave she is.

"Students, parents, guests," she says. At first, she stands stiffly, staring vaguely into the distance. But as she goes on, she warms and softens. She looks from one side to the other, even moves between them as she speaks. "Prom is a celebration for every student at James Madison High. It's a celebration of our achievements and of our potential as we move toward our futures. It's a celebration for all of us. *All*."

Mrs. Greene jumps up. She doesn't need a megaphone to be heard now that the crowd has quieted. "I want to remind everyone that prom is not a school-sponsored event! Principal Hawkins refuses to fund the prom—"

"It's not in the budget," Principal Hawkins interjects. "Our textbooks are ten years old, and our technology is even older!"

As if he said nothing, Mrs. Greene goes on, "This is a social event that *we*, the *parents*, host, and as such, we're entitled to decide who may and may not attend! We are not going to let the government or the ACLU tell us what to do!"

"We're not the ACLU," Dee Dee cries. She waves at the rabble behind her. "This is the touring cast of *Godspell*, and—"

"My son will not be forced to go to a homosexual prom!" some mom shouts, cutting Dee Dee right off.

"It's not a homosexual prom," Alyssa says. "It's an inclusive prom!"

"Will there be homosexuals there or not?"

"Yes," Alyssa concedes.

Barry "Mr. Pecker" Glickman jumps up, tossing his sign. "And so what if there are? There's nothing wrong with being gay. Look at me! I'm an internationally known thespian, a Drama Desk winner, and gay as a bucket of wigs!"

A gasp fills the room. Like, a literal, coordinated gasp of horror. Edgewater is in the middle of nowhere, but it's not like it's the fourteenth century or anything. We get *Drag Race* here.

And there are quietly gay people in town. Gay people who have "roommates" or "friends," who don't hold hands in public and definitely didn't go out and get married once Indiana joined the rest of the country (dead last) and legalized marriage equality.

But nowhere in Edgewater—like, ever—has anybody jumped up in the middle of a school assembly and yelled that they were gay.

Ever.

Actually, I don't think I've ever said it like that myself. On my channel, I said I was in love with a girl. To my parents, I didn't have to say anything, or to my nan. Or . . . wow, I came out freshman year, but I've literally never told anyone I'm gay. And now that I've heard that collective gasp, I may never.

Barry steps into the center ring and looks around. "Emma! Where are you?"

The bench does not, conveniently, fall into a sinkhole and take me with it. Everyone's looking, and it's not like I can pretend to be somebody besides the lesbian in question. After all, I'm the only girl here in plaid flannel and sensible shoes. Slowly, I raise my hand.

Flinging himself toward me, Barry throws out his arms. "Look at this poor creature! Wasting away under your judgment! Your criticism! Your off-the-rack offerings!"

Emboldened, Dee Dee jumps forward. In fact, she jumps in a way that I'm not entirely sure she hasn't practiced. "We didn't come here to make a scene!" Her head pivots, and she addresses Shelby, who has her phone raised to take in all the action. "Darling, if you're going to take pictures, make sure you hashtag 'broadway crashes the prom,' hashtag 'dee dee allen,' hashtag 'no filter'—"

"This! Is not about us," Barry says, flinging an arm around me. He is solid and he is *strong*. He also smells like really expensive soap. He turns toward most of the senior class, their parents, and two reporters to declare, "This is about you and prying open your tiny little minds!"

Nick's dad—recognizable as such because he wears his son's jersey, for real—stands and bellows, "Just who the hell do you think you are?"

"We," Barry says and—hand to god—places a palm on his chest like this is the Pledge of Allegiance, "are liberal actors from New York!"

Tilting toward Nan, I murmur, "Why didn't he just say Satan and his minions?"

"And we represent liberty and justice for all," Dee Dee adds. "We're here for America!"

"This is not America," Mrs. Greene says. "This is Edgewater, Indiana! We have morals here. We have a way of life that we're proud of! We believe in God and country, and we believe there's a right way and a wrong way!"

Before this turns into an all-out brawl between Mrs. Greene and Dee Dee, and honestly, it's looking like that might still happen, Principal Hawkins steps between them. "Ladies, ladies, can we please, just for a moment, hear from the person this affects most?"

What the what?! I didn't come here to talk! I came because Alyssa asked me to and because I was curious about the pro-testors. Because it was kind of nice to see that there were more people on my side than my nan, my girl, and the principal. It's one thing to talk to my YouTube channel. Those comments are nice, and focused on my guitar work, and safe on the other side of my laptop screen! I don't want to stand up and talk to people who look like they'd bite me if they weren't afraid of catching the gay!

Principal Hawkins reclaims the megaphone and approaches me with it. "This is Emma Nolan. An honor roll student since freshman year. She's a very talented musician, and she's been a model student here for four years. Emma *is* James Madison, and now she'd like to go to the prom. Emma, can you tell us what this means to you?"

I feel the fire of a thousand stares on me. I feel the weight of a thousand churches on me. I feel the crushing grip of an actor around my shoulders.

My parents aren't here; they threw me away. But everybody else's parents are here in their place. They stare at me, stony. Their eyes are gray and angry. Their hands are folded tight, so tight, their knuckles are white. Can't Principal Hawkins see how much they hate me? Doesn't he realize that it doesn't mat-ter what I say?

Apparently not. He stands beside me and looks at me ex-pectantly. Barry gives me an encouraging shake. I steal a look at Alyssa, but I can't linger. Her mother is here. The town is here. I'm not alone right now, but right this second, I feel it.

My voice warbles when I speak into the megaphone. And

hang on to your butts, you're never going to believe the stirring and inspirational thing I say. Are you ready? Here we go:

"I just want to go to prom like everybody else."

It's the least profound thing I could have possibly said. And at the same time, I may as well have thrown a beehive into a hair salon. The screaming. Oh my god, the *screaming*.

"You can't make us have a homosexual prom!"

"She's here! She's queer! Get used to it!"

"This school cannot condone discrimination!"

And once again, it's everybody howling, nobody listening. As I watch them tear into each other—and some of the Broadway people start to sing selections from *Hamilton*—I just stare. All of this because of me. I am a seed of Chaos. Heck, maybe I'm the Red Rider of the Apocalypse.

Hilariously, if I am, that means that literally nobody in my hometown got called home to Jesus. They all got left behind.

A hysterical laugh escapes me, projected by the megaphone. Pushing it away, I shake my head. I think I say *thanks* to Barry, and *I'm sorry* to Principal Hawkins, but I slip out the side door and into the cool night air. As nice as it is to finally have people on my side, I've got to get out of here. Pulling my phone from my pocket, I text Alyssa, So that was fun!

She pings me back instantly. I'm so sorry.

So am I. But that, I keep to myself.

10. Mama Who Raised Me

ALYSSA

The ride home from the meeting isn't quiet. I almost wish it were. It would be so much easier to sit next to a mother who stews in silence. It would be so much easier to believe I haven't disappointed her in every single way.

"And what was that, with *The prom is a celebration for us all?* Honestly, Alyssa, I raised you better than that."

"Actually," I say, "you raised me to be a strong woman. To stand up for what I believe in."

"I raised you to be a good Christian!"

My stomach hurts, and it's telling my brain to shut up. *Shutting up doesn't mean agreement,* it wheedles. Thomas More died to prove that. Then again, Thomas More *died* to prove that. I mumble, "And I think that's what I'm being. Love thy neighbor as you love thyself?"

Mom turns to look at me so sharply, her neck pops. There's fury in her eyes; it sizzles all the way to the tips of her blowout and threatens to jump off and start a wildfire. Every word that leaps from her lips is an ember ready to catch. "I'm not telling you to hate that girl. Hate the sin, love the sinner. It would be loving the sin to encourage her to swan around our prom with some out-of-town girl. Especially after she dragged those crazies from New York here to embarrass us—"

"She didn't invite them, Mom!"

Shaking with anger, Mom clutches the steering wheel and buries the needle on the speedometer. Our car shakes, too, when we hit seventy-five. It's twelve years old and on its third set of tires. Somehow, my mother manages to explode with rage but also drive in a perfectly straight line. "Oh, don't give me that, Alyssa. She all but begged outsiders to get involved in this when she mocked our rules on the internet!"

"Because you guys made them just to keep her from going to the prom! She's one person, Mom. What does it hurt?"

"What does it hurt? Everything. You can't compromise your values or you compromise who you are! If we let that girl come to the prom, then what's next? Boys dressing up like girls to get into the locker room? One sin leads to another, and that leads to damnation!"

I flinch when she says these things, because . . . look, I always knew that my mother would have a hard time with me being queer. But I didn't realize how deep that . . . I don't want to call it *hatred*. I don't want to call my mother a homophobe and a transphobe, but, god, it's all right there on the surface.

"None of those things are going to happen! Leaving gay people alone hurts *nothing*."

"Oh no?" Mom counters furiously. "Gay marriage is suddenly legal and your father leaves?"

"He left for a weather girl in Kansas!"

"After the Supreme Court told him that the bonds of marriage didn't matter! They made us compromise our values, and one compromise leads to— Alyssa, one day, you will understand. You're in a broken home right now. You're confused."

"Mom, I'm not confused."

She waves that off, the rationalization and denial working overtime. "It's all right. When your father gets back, we'll go to counseling at the church. Pastor Jimenez is a wonderful man, it will be good for all of us. You'll see."

I scrub my face with both hands. I'm trying, so hard, to keep my mother together. But it's starting to feel like keeping her together is tearing me apart. My dad isn't coming back, and I'm not even allowed to be angry about that. She doesn't give me any room or any breath to feel my *own* feelings about the fact that he started a whole new family. He replaced me with a brand-new baby, and I only know that because his cousin messaged me on Facebook!

Instead, I have to spend all my time making *her* feel better, keeping *her* from any more upset or heartbreak. I'm three months away from eighteen, four months away from college. If she hasn't gotten over this by then, this *obsession* with perfection, this certainty that she can make everything right and my father will come running back, am I going to keep propping her up?

Or am I going to be like nice Ms. Reynolds, who sells tomatoes on a table in her front yard and pretends like Ms. Gloria's not her partner? Am I going to ask Emma to lie for the rest of her life, just to be with me?

Emma's ready to stop lying *now*. How long until she decides I'm not worth the fight?

How long does my mother's happiness have to come first?

Swallowing hard, I look out at the fields I love, newly furrowed for the year. The rows are so neat, so orderly. They're nothing but lines drawn in the earth, but in a few weeks, they'll announce spring with brand-new shoots.

New life, new greenness, stretching out in every direction. I want to be part of that orderly pattern. I want to fit in, in my own town, in my own house. And I want it as I *am*. Not the way Mom wishes me to be.

"We can go to counseling all day long, Mom, but I'm not going to change my mind about this. Prom should be for everybody."

My mother pushes her jaw forward; she always does this when she's beating on a problem and trying to solve it. "I don't know where you got this wild hair, Alyssa."

"I took an oath," I say firmly. "I'm the president of student council. Not president of the students I pick and choose. I didn't think the basketball players deserved new jerseys this year, but I voted to get them anyway. It's important to them! And this is important to Emma."

"Emma, Emma, Emma," my mother mocks, waving a hand. "She must be loving all of this attention. Those people do. I mean, look at that disgraceful display tonight!"

"But that was them, not her."

"It was *for* her, so what's the difference? You'll never convince me she didn't orchestrate that!"

I can't remember ever raising my voice to my mother, so it startles us both when I rail at her. "It never would have happened if there wasn't something to protest! And I bet you a million dollars they're going to *keep* protesting until *we* change!"

"Alyssa, enough!"

My mother's voice is a blade. It slices between us, severing our conversation. Her perfect veneer falters, revealing all the cracks underneath. She's so close to breaking. We pass beneath a traffic light. Her face glows green for a moment, then goes dark. And when the dark comes again, everything's smoothed back into place.

"So, tell me about this John Cho," she says, as if we weren't just arguing. As if she can hit reset on our lives and move forward in a more pleasant direction. "If you met him at Model UN, then he must be smart. Not as smart as my baby girl, but smart."

"Mom," I say, warning.

"You have to be careful," she goes on. "Boys don't like it when you're *too* smart. But look at that face. That beautiful face. That will distract him every time."

"Mom, I canceled, okay? You changed the rules about outside dates, so I called it off."

With an expression of pure dismay, Mom cries out, "Alyssa, honey! Why would you do that? I told you that didn't apply to you."

"It should have," I say flatly.

It's all written on her face: this ruins everything. There's a perfect night to be had, and it has to be had with me on my date's arm. For a moment, it looks like she might cry. But then she finds some well of strength and waves off this obstacle like an errant fly.

"There's still time. Call him back! Hey, do you know what? I'm so glad we went to Edinburgh to get your dress. You're going to outshine everyone there. It's just a shame you refused to run for the court. Kaylee will probably win now, and she's not half as pretty as you are."

Carefully, I ask, "Does this means prom's not canceled? For sure?"

My mother's laughter, light and airy, fills the car. She glances over at me, her smile perfectly fixed, her teeth perfectly white. She's so perfect, she sounds like the fairy godmother from a Disney movie when she says, "As if I would ever keep my own daughter from her senior prom."

Wary, I look at her. Did I change her mind? I don't know why, but I'm afraid to ask. It would be such good news if she just decided to give in. But I honestly can't tell if this is surrender or if her break with reality just became permanent. I say nothing.

Mom reaches over to take my hand and squeeze it. "I'd love to take pictures in front of the fireplace and under the swinging oak. Is he taller than you? If he's not, it's fine. You can wait to put on your heels. Do you know when he's going to pick you up?"

"Mom, I told you I canceled," I say, schooling my voice to sound normal, as if any of this is normal. "He's not coming."

"And I told you to call him," Mom says, wriggling happily in her seat.

I start to argue. Then I realize that it's foolish to argue about my imaginary date's imaginary social calendar. It's easier to be quiet, and unsettled, and just feed my mother the nodding agreement she wants. It changes nothing, but it brings a bit of peace to the ride home.

For now, peace is good enough.

11. Wouldn't It Be Loverly?

EMMA

For some reason, Nan wants to talk to the Broadway people.

So we follow their tour bus to the Comfort Inn by the highway. I'm relieved that they didn't end up at the Knights Inn on the other side of the highway. That one rents by the hour; truckers love it.

The tour bus is parked at the back of the lot, and half the *Godspell* people are gathered in knots just outside. Two of the guys tangle in each other's arms—I don't think they're trying to keep warm, either.

Moving through them, I watch in amazement as one of the girls grabs the curve of one foot and raises it above her head. She just perches there on the other foot, arching her back and carrying on a conversation at the same time.

"Put your eyes back in your head," Nan says, amused, and ushers me inside. The foyer is more of the same, only this time with a guy sitting in a girl's lap on the couch by the front door, and excited conversations exploding next to the luggage racks.

But we're here for two specific Broadway people; they're

standing at the front desk. Nan waves a hand, calling out, "Mr. Glickman! Ms. Allen!"

Barry stops mid-monologue at the hotel clerk—surprise, surprise, there's no sauna and no room service at the Edgewater, Indiana, Comfort Inn. Also, no suites. I mean, it's only three stories high—what did they expect? He smooths the front of his jacket and walks toward us.

"Emma, honey," he says, and instead of shaking my hand, he captures it between his and squeezes. There might even be a little bow involved; I'm not quite sure. "What are you doing here?"

"We wanted to thank all of you," Nan says. She steps ever so slightly in front of me, a tiny, bingo-playing wall of protection. "I want to thank you, for coming all this way for my Emma. She's had a rough row to hoe the past couple years."

"Farm metaphors," Dee Dee says, turning her roller bag and snapping the handle closed with precision. "How charming!"

Barry lets go of my hand and nods. "I never got to go to prom. Okay, correction, I went to fourteen proms—just not my own. And I—"

"We," Dee Dee interjects.

Barry gives her a look. "We couldn't let that happen to you. Not in this day and age."

"It's tough out here for this little girl," Nan says, ruffling my hair like I'm a toddler. Slightly embarrassed, I lean away. If she moves on to squeezing cheeks next, she's going to have to grab Barry. Who knows? He might even be into that.

I say, "I just don't understand why this is such a big deal."

"It's ignorance," Dee Dee announces with certainty. "It's backwater ignorance! These hayseeds don't learn because they don't *want* to learn."

Even though I live here, even though I mostly hate living here, my hackles rise. Dee Dee's from New York, a magical fairyland where apparently you can make a living pretending to be other people onstage, and also, public transportation actually exists.

She's standing here talking about ignorance when she doesn't even know that we have no hayseeds in Indiana.

We don't grow much wheat here. No wheat, no hayseeds, hello. We grow corn and soybeans; we're dairy farmers and hog farmers. (Also, we export limestone and natural gas. You're welcome.) It's one thing if she calls us rednecks. People around here do get the backs of their necks sunburned working in the fields. But hayseeds? Not so much.

And I can't even believe I'm mentally defending this place, but I am. I live here. I know all our faults. If I want to talk Hoosier trash, well, bring the chicken and noodles on mashed potatoes, because I will. *My* trash is *accurate*. Dee Dee, however, is about to get an attitude adjustment, courtesy of this baby gayseed.

"Can I steal this delightful little sugarplum for just a minute?" Barry asks.

Nan looks him over, then glances at me. Touching her nose, she points. "I better be able to see you at all times."

So much for schooling Dee Dee. I'm still itching to mouth off to her, but my temper fades the farther we get from her. Barry and I end up in matching green chairs by the cookie table—after he shoos a couple of chorus kids out of his way. They look at him like he's a god. I'm guessing a Roman one, who likes his feasts and libations.

A tray of chocolate chip and snickerdoodle cookies sits beneath a sign that welcomes anyone to have a bite. No tongs, though. If you want one, you're gonna have to grab it with your grubby hand like everybody else.

Despite this, Barry takes a cookie and breaks it. He offers me half and fixes me with a sympathetic smile.

"I've been exactly where you are," he says, and his eyes are so kind as he glances toward Nan. "I mean, at least you've got your mother?"

"Actually," I tell him, "that's my grandmother. She took me in when Mom and Dad kicked me out."

"How did *that* happen?"

"Nan says she must have dropped Dad on his head too many times when he was a baby." I shrug and offer a game smile.

But instead of laughing along, Barry murmurs the most sympathetic sound. The regret on his face is so real and so present that I tear up. He's still Mr. Pecker in my head, but he's a better version of him. Sweet, sincere.

Abandoning his half of the cookie, he rests his chin on his hand just so, then says, "That's rough, kiddo. And . . . I've been there, too."

"I'm sorry."

"Me too." He looks to the distance, but then snaps back to the present. "But I'm here to tell you, people like us? We get to choose our family. And when we see each other, across the room or across the country, we care. Instead of your uncle who tells racist jokes at Thanksgiving, you get me now."

"The uncle who pickets my school?"

"Honey, the auntie who's going to change your life." With a flourish, he smiles; he snaps.

He is seriously the gayest person I've ever met, and I've been to third base with my girlfriend. I guess I should say, he's the most stereotypically gay person I've ever met? He's the queeniest person I've ever met? I don't even know!

I might be showing my own internalized homophobia right now. Because Barry looks perfectly comfortable in his skin, and I'm perched on a hotel chair with a cold cookie in my claws, a gargoyle too basic to make the grade for the church bell tower.

"And do you know what?" Barry says, leaning toward me and lowering his voice. "There's a way out of here. I watched the rest of the videos on your channel. You're talented, Emma. There's always room for talented people—session singing, background singing, overdubbing tuneless blondes in yet another *Mamma Mia* sequel? I'm such a petty bitch, pretend I didn't say that last one."

I'm surprised by my own smile, my own sudden laughter. He's saying all the things I want to hear. Here's somebody who's completely, totally on my side. Who's been through what I'm going through now. Who made it to the other side. When they say *it gets better*, this is what they mean.

"Barry . . . can I call you Barry?" I say, testing the weight of his name on my tongue when he nods. "I really appreciate you coming all this way. But after tonight . . . I'm not sure it's a good idea to keep pushing. You saw how mad all the parents are. And when you showed up at school today, you literally interrupted a death threat in progress."

"But, Emma! That's *exactly* why we're here!"

"You don't think this is going to make it worse?"

Picking up his chair by the arms, Barry turns it toward me and drops it with a heavy thump. He catches my hands again. "Absotively not. We won't let that happen. Between me and Dee Dee, this is going to be the most watched prom in the country. They wouldn't dare."

"That's really nice of you, but we still don't know if there's going to be a prom. And also?" I roll my shoulders ruefully. "Even if there is, I don't think my girlfriend's going to come."

Barry looks like he's about to say something sassy and possibly inappropriate. He thinks better of it and rubs his hands together. His voice lilts, almost like he's singing, when he asks, "Who's your girlfriend?"

Boy, do I appreciate the gobsmacked look on his face when I say, "Alyssa Greene, the student council president. Her mom's the head of the PTA; she's the one who hates my guts."

Scandalized, Barry asks, "Does she know?"

"Nooooo," I say. "Not about me and not about her daughter, and she's not going to find out until Alyssa's ready, got it?"

"I'm here as an agent of Cupid, not a sower of discord, darling." Barry nods firmly at that, then says, "You know what? You work on your date, and I'll work on everything else. Leave it to me, Emma. There *will* be a prom, and it will be perfect. I'll take care of your flowers, your hair, your shoes—you have a dress?"

I stammer, "Uh, no," but fail to say I had no intention of wearing a dress.

"Oh, sweetheart, I've got so much work to do. Where's the nearest Saks?"

"We don't have one."

He shudders but amends, "Macy's?"

I shake my head. "Sorry. We have a Walmart?"

"Oh good god, you're going to prom, not a hoedown. All right. Breathe. Center. Exhale. Good." He claps his hands and ends his impromptu meditation session. "No Saks, no problem. Tony Award–winning costume designer Gregg Barnes owes me a favor or two. I'll have him FedEx a selection and bring them by."

"To school?"

"Your humble abode, Emma." Barry considers, then asks, "If your grandmother won't have a problem with a middle-aged man prancing around your bedroom."

We both glance at her at the same time. She's petting one of the young picketers; his long, golden hair does look irresistible. I say, "She's gonna make us leave the door open and keep both feet on the floor."

"I'll do my best," Barry jokes.

My cell phone gurgles with a school alert. I pull it from my pocket, but I don't look at it. My throat is dry and my heart is still. I tell Barry, "That's something from the school."

"Read it," he says. "If it's a battle, we must prepare. Wouldn't want to show up to a slap fight barehanded."

Unlocking the screen, I touch the notification. It takes a minute for my mail to load. Signal reception is hit or miss around here because of all the limestone, and also because we live in the middle of nowhere. The screen finally flashes white, and there it is. A letter from the PTA.

"Regarding this year's prom," I say shakily, then read on. "After much consideration and consultation with friends, family, and the community, the James Madison PTA has decided to move forward with plans to host the prom at its original date and time. We will be in touch with more information as necessary. Thank you for your passionate advocacy. We are proud of our students and our class of 2019 Golden Weevils. Sincerely, Elena Greene, PTA president."

"We did it," Barry says, so quiet it's almost a whisper. Then he leaps up and shouts into the other room. "Dee Dee! Non-equity cast of *Godspell*! We did it! Emma's going to the prom!"

A roar fills the hotel foyer. Jazz hands and kicks-ball-change (kick-ball-changes?) break out everywhere. The news travels fast, shouted out the sliding front doors with ecstatic glee. There are so many bright, delighted faces around me that I can't help but laugh. This is a mob scene I can appreciate.

"Yay *us!*" Dee Dee shouts, throwing her arms over her head.

Nan raises an eyebrow. "More like yay Emma."

"It can be them," I concede. "Everything changed when they got here."

With that, Barry sweeps Dee Dee up in a very choreographed waltz (I'm guessing—how should I know? This is Indiana 2019, not Versailles 1719—although there is a Versailles, Indiana, and guess how many of those *S*s and *L*s we pronounce. Spoiler: all of them).

As people cheer around me and burst into song—they've been here a minute, and I've already noticed that happens a lot—I bask in stunned silence. My phone weighs a million pounds, but I'm as light as air. I'm going to prom.

I'm going to prom!

12. Something Begun

ALYSSA

I push open my car door, and Emma jumps in.

Throwing my arms around her, I kiss her. I kiss her hard and fast; I kiss her softly. I kiss her until our lips are sticky and my windows are fogged. She tastes like bubble gum and electricity, a sweet summer storm that rolls through me and rumbles on and on.

Even though we're still parked in her grandmother's driveway, I kiss her again and again, apologies and promises, greetings, but no goodbyes for once. Not yet. Not tonight.

When Emma pulls back for a breath, she presses her brow to mine. Her fingers slip through my hair; I shiver. She's familiar and constant and untouchable all at the same time, and I feed her my relief on soft caresses that fall on her skin. We've been so far away lately—I was afraid we might not snap back together, but we do.

We fit, my hands in hers, my lips on hers, my heart against hers. A little trill runs through my chest, and I'm dizzy for a moment. She makes me dizzy.

"How'd you manage a prison break?" Emma asks, her lips teasing in a smile.

"Tunneled out behind a picture of Ruby Rose on my wall."

Laughter fills my car, and she hugs me fiercely. When she pulls back, she leans her head against the headrest. She plays with my fingers between hers. Her fingertips are rough from playing the guitar; they create their own kisses on the palm of my hand. "Seriously, though?" she asks.

"Seriously? Her manager at the Red Stripe threatened to write her up if she missed any more shifts."

"Yikes," Emma says, furrowing her brow. "I guess when you get into the grocery deli game, it's hard to get out."

My laugh is soft; my eye-rolling amused instead of annoyed. Even though my mother has made Emma's life exponentially harder, she doesn't hold it against me. She's not cruel about her, and sometimes—especially lately—I really feel like she kind of has the right to be.

My mother is a complicated disaster, but she's my complicated disaster. And she's really all I have. My grandparents retired to New Mexico; my only aunt lives in Des Moines. They exist solely in Christmas and birthday cards, on Facebook and text message. My dad . . . well, you know all about my dad.

"I've been thinking," I say, and my skin goes hot as soon as I say it. "The prom is back on, and obviously, that wouldn't be the case if Mom hadn't softened a little—"

"What, you don't think it was the Broadway invasion that changed her mind?"

"Emma."

"They're doing a number at the truck rally this weekend, just to make a point. Can you *imagine* the looks in that crowd? *Sunday, Sunday, Sunday! We'll sell you the seat, but you'll only need the edge, edge, edge—and a taste for show tunes.* I tried to warn them."

Covering my face with my hand, I shake my head, "Why, even? They got what they came for."

"The show must go on?" Emma says, more like a question. She shrugs, and then her face changes—her tone, too. To something soft, almost wondrous. "Barry's calling in a favor from a costume designer. For my outfit."

"You're on a first-name basis now?"

Emma nods, her dark hair bobbing, her glasses slipping down her nose. "Apparently I am. And I think his idea of formal wear for me doesn't match *my* idea, but . . . we talked for a long time last night. It was really nice."

Guilt coils inside me. She's doing this all alone. Worse, this is all my mother's fault *and* she's doing this alone. Mr. Glickman and Ms. Allen seem a little . . . intense, but I guess I can't blame Emma for embracing them. I make myself smile and ask, "Was it?"

With her gaze out the window, something plays out on Emma's features. It's like she catches herself up in a memory. She sounds wistful when she says, "Yeah, it was. It's like he's the very first person who really *gets* me."

My smile falters. "Ouch."

"You know what I mean," Emma says. All of a sudden, she's moving, filling my car with flying hands and animation. I haven't seen her this excited since she found out the new *Sabrina* was going to be freaky-scary instead of goofy-silly.

"He's just *out* there," she goes on. "His mom pushed him out, too. And he said that people like us, we get to choose our families. We get to choose the people around us, and I never thought about that before. If family is love, then the people we love are family."

I'm not sure why, but unease snakes through me, low through my belly. I feel like I'm holding on to a balloon too tight, afraid that it'll slip from my grasp. I interrupt this train of thought and say, "I don't want to change the subject or anything, but I do . . . I mean, so you know, I do still want us to do it—go to prom together."

She stops short. "I thought that was already settled."

"It is, it was!" I say. "I just didn't know, with everything that's happened . . . if, I don't know, maybe you'd changed your mind."

With that, Emma leans back and looks at me. Really looks at me. "You realize I'm the only thing that *hasn't* changed in all of this, right? I didn't ask for your mother to turn this into a referendum on my personhood. And I didn't ask for Broadway to picket the school. I didn't ask for any of this."

"No, of course you didn't!" I hold up my hands. "Please, I don't want to fight."

"I don't either." Emma looks so disappointed, but then she catches my hands. "And you know what? I don't want to start a riot. I don't want to blaze a trail or be a symbol—and I don't care what other people think. I just want to dance with you."

When the tears spring up, they catch me by surprise. *That's all I want, too,* I want to say. To dance together, and let the world melt away, and to just feel right about it. To feel no fear. I love Emma so much it hurts, and I hate that the way I've been loving her hurts her, too. Finally, I say, "I just want to hold you."

"And I don't want to let you go," she says. Tears glimmer in her eyes, too. "Two people swaying, that's it. Nobody knows how to dance anymore anyway. So it'll be you and me, shuffling awkwardly to music nobody was ever supposed to dance to. I don't know why that scares them so much, but I don't care, Alyssa. All I care about is you."

I turn away to sniff. I'm a gross crier, and when I kiss her after this, I don't want to slime her. "I promise you. When we get there, it's going to be just you and me and a song."

Emma falls into my arms again, and I hold her so tight. I rub my cheek against her hair and squeeze until I feel her exhale a breath. It's not right that something this good, this *perfect*, can cause so much trouble. No—that other people let something this good, this perfect, bother *them*.

A soft rain opens up, and the hush of drops spilling over the roof of my car does that thing that Emma wants—it makes the world melt away. Right now, here in the dark, in the mist, beneath the fall of rain, there is no world, just this. Just now.

Just us.

13. Razzle, Also Some Dazzle, Plus, Pound Cake

EMMA

I hear Barry and Dee Dee on the porch before they knock on the door.

More specifically, I hear Dee Dee doing something that sounds suspiciously like a few steps of tap dancing. Then, when she knocks on the door, it's bright and strident. I leap up from the bright yellow lounger in the living room to answer.

"I was expecting them to be fashionably late," Nan says, pulling out a bread knife to slice the cake she made. The whole house smells like sugar and vanilla, and even though I'm nervous, I open the door with a smile.

"Nous sommes arrivés," Dee Dee announces, stepping through the door like a showgirl. She catches me up in her manicured hands, pressing her cheek to mine and mwahing right next to my ear. When she lets go, I practically spin across the floor. She's been in my house for less than ten seconds and I'm already out of breath.

A clothing rack comes through the door next, Barry pushing it from behind. His perfect skin is slightly pink, and when he gets in, he pulls a handkerchief from his pocket and daubs it across his face. When he finishes, he literally closes his eyes, takes a breath, and then comes back to the present.

"Emma!" he says, lighting up. He doesn't spin me across the room, thankfully. He just grabs my hands and squeezes them. "How are you, darling?"

Overwhelmed. Excited. Slightly nauseated? I say none of those things, because none of them answer the question. I'm all of them, and more. I feel like a weathervane, spinning toward ecstasy, then back toward despair. So I offer a smile instead and lead him inside. "I'm good, thank you, how are you?"

"Recuperating," Dee Dee answers for him. She turns, as if looking for somewhere to perch. We have a couch, a love seat, a rocking chair, and the yellow lounger, but Dee Dee seems out of sorts. Finally, she manages to arrange herself against the fireplace. Placing a hand dramatically over her heart she says, "No one appreciated our performance at the rally. They threw things!"

"Did they really?" Nan asks, hiding a smile.

"They did! Do you know how many people would pay good money to see us in New York?"

"It was probably the up-and-down weather," Nan says. "People get a little loopy when spring is almost here. Would you like some refreshments?" She ferries thick yellow slices of pound cake onto paper plates. I can't wait to see what Dee Dee does with disposable dishes.

Dee Dee peeks at the cake and quickly shifts her attention away. "I couldn't possibly," she says. Then, just as quickly, she reverses herself. "But it would be so terribly rude to decline. Just a tiny slice for me?"

"I want to get these out of the garment bags for Emma," Barry says. "Which way to the boudoir?"

"Uh, if you mean my bedroom, it's this way," I say, gesturing toward the hallway.

Barry puts my hand on the rack and walks off toward my room. I guess he's about done driving this thing around. Amused, I pull it along behind me. It's incredibly heavy, and I can hear things scratching and shaking behind the thick vinyl bags. My guess is rhinestones. At least, I hope that's all it is.

"Oh, I recognize this," Barry says as he sashays into my room. "This is where you record your videos!"

I still can't believe he bothered to watch them. With a shy smile, I sit down on my bed and say dryly, "Yep, this is where the magic happens."

"Well, believe you me," he says, turning to the rack, "it's about to get one thousand percent more magical in here, starting now!"

"You know," I say quickly, "maybe we could mix it up a little. I was thinking a vintage tux, some high-tops . . ."

Appalled, Barry turns to me. "Could we? Yes. Should we? Dear god, no. Sweetheart, I'm begging here. Let me dress you for the prom."

"Okay," I say. I mean, he's from New York. He definitely knows more about fashion than I do. Folding my hands, pressing my knees together, I nod at him encouragingly and wait.

Barry unzips the first garment bag, then throws it back like he's revealing a new piece of art. I recoil, because for a second, it looks like whatever's in there is going to shoot out and stab me with a million little icicles.

When *fight or flight* fades to *slightly anxious in my own skin,* I see that it's a red spangly dress covered with rows upon rows of dangling crystals. The dress shimmies when he pulls it free; it sounds like a hundred whispers all at once when it moves.

"Wow," I say, stunned.

Barry leans in. "Good wow or bad wow?"

"Just wow."

I hate to say no, because it's obviously gorgeous. And I don't want him to think I'm not trying here, but there's no way I'm going to prom in a red hot jazz baby dress like that. It's forty-two inches of va-voom violation of the dress code, and the only accessory I can think to wear with it would be a machine gun. All things considered, that might come off as a tiny bit aggro.

Finally, I come up with something I can say that isn't wildly ungrateful. "It's a little flashy for me."

"Fair enough," he says, and *whoosh!* He flings off another garment bag to reveal a white gown with black ribbon at the ankles, and the waist, and the neck. And ruffles, whoa, so many ruffles at the neck.

It definitely covers all of the body parts I'm required to cover—and then some. The sleeves puff out at the shoulders and taper to tight wristlets. Barry waggles his brows at me. "There's a matching hat, three feet wide, white ostrich plumes for days."

I laugh. "That's just daring all the roosters around here to attack."

At that, Barry chuckles. In the other room, I hear Dee Dee

belting a few lines and Nan singing something back in her crow-like rattle. She's the worst singer I know, but she loves doing it more than anyone I know, too. My grandmother is out there bonding with this Broadway invasionette over pound cake and . . . what sounds like "Swing Low, Sweet Chariot"??

All the tension that's in me, that surrounds me, melts away. It's okay if I don't love this dress; there's another one right behind it. It's okay if I'm an ordinary girl from an ordinary place. Barry makes me feel like there's more to me than this bedroom, this town, this moment. It's easy to get caught up in his enthusiasm, and you know what? I'm gonna let myself.

It's the first time in weeks that I've genuinely laughed. And breathed. And worried about nothing except what frilly Lovecraftian confection might be in the next bag. My house is so much bigger now. Fuller and brighter, somehow. It's just . . . alive. I can't remember the last time my life felt . . . full.

Barry reveals the next dress with a slow flourish. It's pink and fitted, not really me at all. But this one, at least, looks like a dress I could wear to a high school prom. Or to a midday business meeting with a select group of venture capitalists and tech gurus. Easing the hanger free, Barry says, "This one, you have to try on. It's something special."

"Okay," I say. Why not?

"I'll wait for you in the living room. But don't make me wait too long or you'll meet my drag alter ego, Carol Channing Tatum."

"Is that supposed to make me *not* want that?" I ask with a laugh.

He points imperiously. "Go. Now."

With that, I duck down the hall to our bathroom. Stripping out of my flannels and tee, I pull the dress over my head. It's strangely heavy, and I feel packed into it. I never wear clothes this tight.

Looking into the mirror, I try to smooth and flatten . . . and then I try to scoop up my boobs so they sit front and center in this thing. The wide straps cover a lot of my shoulders, but not everything. It's so much skin. It's so revealing.

I have never wanted to be a lacy girl. There's nothing wrong with it—Alyssa is all soft frills and fitted everything, everyday heels and skirts that range from ankle to knee. Her makeup is always soft, mascara framing her big brown eyes, lipstick teasing out the perfect bow of her lips. I love a lacy girl.

But I'm not one. I feel like my joints are ten times too big to walk around in a dress like this. As I slip out of the bathroom and down the hallway, I'm Godzilla in Gucci, tromping through Tokyo Fashion Week.

In the living room, Barry laughs with Nan and Dee Dee. They're waiting to see the dress on me. To be part of my big makeover scene. That's how this works, right? I get a fairy godfather, a glittering gown, glass slippers, a ticket to the ball . . .

I tentatively make my way into the room, and all eyes turn to me. Nervously, I ask, "What do you think?"

"We're getting there," Dee Dee says, unhooking herself from the hearth and handing off her cake to Barry. "Good shoulders, terrible posture. Posture is half the battle, Emma. It rights so many wrongs, makes C cups of so many barely Bs . . ." Clasping my shoulders, Dee Dee looks me in the face and says, "Zazz."

Uh . . . what?

"That's what's missing," she says, whirling around me. She pulls my shoulders back and presses a hand in the middle of my spine. "Breathe in, from the diaphragm."

I take a breath, and I don't say anything. Dee Dee moves in a flash, adjusting my posture, even tipping my chin up with a quick flash of fingers. When she stops in front of me, she stares into my eyes for a long moment and says, "We need to see it in your eyes."

"You want me to smize?"

Crisply, Dee Dee steps into a pose. She's Wonder Woman without the bracelets, suddenly taller, her shoulders appear broader, taking up angular space in a way that simultaneously reminds me of Picasso and praying mantises. "Zazz is style plus confidence. Now let's see it."

"It's just so . . . pink," I say finally.

That's when Barry leaps to his feet. "Sweetheart, I told you this was special." He tugs a ribbon on the side of the dress. "Spin!"

And like a crazy, out-of-control top, I do. I feel the ribbon unfurl; I spin and spin and suddenly, the pink dress turns blue. I don't even know how it happens. The skirt turns fuller and longer, kissing my knees. The top is softer, the shoulder straps turned to cap sleeves. I'm Katniss freaking Everdeen, and I'm gonna be the last girl standing at prom!

"Look at you," Nan says, admiring.

I am never going to be a lacy girl, and I'm never going to love wearing a dress. But this one? This one I can handle. This one is special. It's magic, and these people are, too.

They're magic in Indiana, and maybe—just maybe—a little bit of me is magic, too.

14. It's Raining on Prom Night

ALYSSA

I am in so much trouble. The countdown to prom is in minutes, and I haven't told my mother yet.

The back of my head still burns from way too long under the space bubble hair dryer at Joan's Curl Up 'n' Dye. I've never had this much Aqua Net or glitter in my hair before. When I reach up to touch it, two things happen: first, it crunches a little beneath my fingers, and second, my mother smacks my hand away.

"I've been peeping at those makeup gals online. They all do this," Joan tells her as she paints my face with another round of foundation. "It's called *wake and baking*."

Choking on my gum, I say nothing. There's not enough money in the world to get me to explain to my mother what that really means. If she doesn't know, she'd demand to know how I do. Existing in 2019 would be the answer, but not one she would appreciate hearing.

What *I* don't appreciate is how I haven't had a moment alone with Mom all day. It's like every single time there's been a breath in her nonstop pre-prom prep list, she's flung herself as far from me as possible. I open my mouth to say one serious thing, and her phone blows up on cue.

Oh, there's a balloon emergency. No, the DJ absolutely cannot deviate from the playlist. What do you mean we don't have a punch monitor?

I glance at my phone, so far away from me on Joan's station. Less than an hour until prom starts and I've said word zero to my mother about my date. My very real date who was, last time she managed to text, being semi-felt-up by Dee Dee Allen after the introduction of something Emma would only call "Nightmare Panties by Feather Boa Constrictor."

Meanwhile, my mother hovers over my shoulder, alternately watching her hairdresser pageantify me and barking voice-to-text orders at Shelby's mother through the phone. She stares into the mirror with fiery intensity. It's like she's measuring my face, over and over. Calculating the angle of my updo and quantifying the looseness of the tendrils that fall against my shoulders.

"Mom," I say, "I was hoping we'd get to talk a little before things got crazy."

Joan lunges in with immaculately spray-tanned hands and orders, "Look up!" before attacking me with more mascara.

"Honey, you don't have to say anything," Mom says, catching my hand before it strays toward my hair again. "Just enjoy this. You won't get another special day like this until your wedding day."

"Amen," Joan says, switching to the other eye.

Mom lowers her voice, like she's being naughty. "And

you'll have to share *that* with your mother-in-law."

From the way Joan laughs, my mother is the funniest woman she's ever met. Maybe she used to be, but I'm pretty sure Joan's laughter is a nod. A tribute to the woman most likely to tip well when all of this is through. "Lord, you're not lying. By the time I got to the altar, I was just about ready to tell Nathan it's me or her!"

"Looks like he chose the right one."

"Well, I still have to put up with her and her god-awful ambrosia salad at Christmas, Thanksgiving, Easter, and Race Day . . ."

Just like that, they're chatting about appropriate food for your Indy 500 party and how men's mothers ruin everything. I'm not even here. I'm just the disembodied doll head being decorated within an inch of its life.

A knot tightens in my stomach. I hold very, very still as Joan coaxes a smoky eye out of a mostly pastel palette, and I try not to frown when my mother chooses the shade of my lipstick.

"It's important," I tell my mother, when Joan turns away to open a tackle box full of cosmetics. That's not a joke. She has the same bright yellow plastic organizer that half the guys in town have rattling around in the beds of their pickup trucks.

Mom holds up a finger. "Hold on; Shelby's mother doesn't know if anybody bought the sherbert."

Because nothing says *classy evening of elegance* like a massive punch bowl full of ginger ale with melted rainbow foam in it. But to be fair, it *is* served at wedding receptions, baby showers, and anniversary parties all over town. The way people fuss over the punch, you'd think it was a recipe handed down across the generations and not copied off a Schweppes label sometime in the last century.

And if I didn't know better, I'd think my mother is deliberately avoiding me. Every time I gather the words in my mind and the courage in my heart, she darts away again. *Stop being paranoid*, I tell myself. *She's like this with every event she plans for school.*

Forty minutes before homecoming last fall, she was hanging—lit-er-ally hanging—from the top of a ladder, trimming the crepe paper streamers in the gym to exactly the same length. She's not going to relax until the last balloon drops and the final fleck of confetti settles on the dance floor. It just feels like she's avoiding me because I've been putting this off for so long.

"Here we are!"

Joan surfaces from the tackle box and puts a plastic dish in my hand. Carefully, she selects a glimmering crystal from the container and dots the back of it with eyelash glue. One after the other, Joan affixes three little gleaming gems at the corner of my eye, then steps back.

Admiring her own handiwork in the mirror, she waves my mother over. Joan mouths, "She's beautiful," and my mother mouths back, "Thank you."

Their pride lasts half a second. Then Mom, with the phone to her ear, pushes the hanger with my dress on it into my hands. Half whispering, she says, "Go on, get changed. We're running out of time, and I want to get some pictures of you."

"Mom, I—"

"Vamoose, Alyssa," she says. And then she gives me a swat

on the butt, like I'm six years old and we're running late for church. Into the phone, she says, "Yes, I'm still here. Did you look in the freezer? Not the cooler, the freezer?"

The salon's bathroom smells like perm solution and vanilla candles. The scent is thick, and it makes me queasy, but I manage to get out of my street clothes and into the overtime gown without incident.

I'm careful not to yank the straps on my dress too hard. For some reason, I remember them being a lot more substantial in the store. Now, they're just thin, jeweled threads that definitely do not meet dress code.

A wash of lavender satin and tulle surrounds me. The full skirt murmurs when I move. A perfect fit. Exactly right. My makeup matches perfectly, even if it is a little thick for my taste. Trying to turn in the tight space, I wobble, and wonder if my hair will shatter if it hits the wall. I'd better not find out.

I wonder what Emma's doing right now. When I Marcoed her last night, she sat her phone on her dresser to stay in frame. All nerves and excitement, Emma's anticipation shone in her bright pink cheeks, and eyes that glittered like Christmas lights. She kept rolling onto her back, then onto her stomach, unable to lie still.

My guess is, she's surrounded by Nan and Mr. Glickman and Ms. Allen, enduring hair and makeup just like me. She told me Mr. Glickman conned her into a dress, but she refused to show it to me. She wanted it to be a surprise. So right now, she's probably counting down the minutes until all the waiting is over. Until it's finally the two of us.

And most of our high school.

And my mother.

Who still doesn't know.

The thing is, I'm trying. I'm really trying! Mom hasn't stopped long enough to breathe, let alone have a heart-to-heart. Everything happened so fast after prom was officially back on that time just slipped from my grasp.

But it's fine. As soon as I'm dressed and the pictures are over, all that's left is the drive to the school. Mom won't be able to get away from me then. I have a semi-thought-out plan. First, I'll turn down the radio. Not all the way, just low enough that she can hear me over it. But not so low that I have to fill the silence all by myself.

Then I'll hold her hand; she loves it when I do that. I think it reminds her that I'm still her baby, even if I'm not a little girl anymore. So yes, I'll hold her hand and I'll start by thanking her. For being my mom. For being funny—she used to be funny, before Dad left, and I know she could be again. For being a part of every big moment in my life, for celebrating them with me.

For loving me.

For loving me unconditionally.

And then I'll just say it. I'll open my mouth, and I will—

"Alyssa!" my mother calls through the door, rapping on it sharply. "What's taking so long? Do you need help with the zipper?"

I want to laugh, but I'm wound too tight. No matter how much I want to convince myself that this will all be okay, I know it won't. Darkness creeps up inside me, and I want to tear off the dress, scrub the makeup off my face. I want to run. But that's not going to happen, so I have to admit this, to myself, so I can move forward:

My mom's not going to pleasantly surprise me with her reaction. I know her. I know how this goes.

At night, when I put my hands together and try to think of something to pray for that isn't selfish, I ask for peace of mind for my mom. For acceptance. Or even tolerance. I sit with this huge secret, praying for divine intervention, because I know I haven't misjudged her.

She's on a razor-thin edge with Dad leaving, yes, that's going to blow up on her, sooner rather than later, yes, but I think—no, I know.

Even if everything were perfect—if my dad had stayed, if Mom were still a housewife and stay-at-home mother instead of a junior deli clerk at the age of forty-eight, my being a lesbian *still wouldn't be okay with her*. She doesn't even have the vocabulary to understand who I am. In her world, in her mind, there's gay and there's *normal*.

And that means, if I'm not straight, I'm not normal.

I wasn't there, exactly, when Emma's parents kicked her out. Slightly before my time. But I've heard the story. She's lain in her bed at Nan's house, with her head in my lap, trying to find some meaning to it. Trying to figure out if her mom and dad actually loved her before, and somehow, she destroyed that by existing . . . or if they never loved her at all. Not really. Not unconditionally.

My mother's love has conditions. I already know the price of admission in the Greene house is perfection. *Normal* perfection.

If mom kicks me out, I have nowhere to go. My grandparents are just as religious as Mom is, maybe even more so. They're yard-sign people, handwritten harangues about whatever moral ills are in the news on any given day. Last June, they had one that said *The rainbow is God's promise, not Satan's flag.* They could have forty-seven extra rooms; there wouldn't be one for me in their house. Not once they knew.

That leaves my dad. My dad, who threw away the life that included me, and got as far from Edgewater as possible. The dad who doesn't call, doesn't write, doesn't pay for my textbook rental or new sneakers. He has a new wife. He has a new baby. If I knocked on his door, what would he say? I bet it would be something like, "I'm so sorry, I thought I canceled my subscription to you."

Things are tight for Emma and Nan, so even if I thought they would take me in, I could never ask. It's too much. Too big.

Call me selfish; maybe I am selfish. But I'm selfish *and* afraid. I've done the research. Forty percent of homeless teens are queer. A quarter of queer kids get kicked out when they come out. It's a long, long summer before college starts in the fall. I mean, at least I have a car. The title's in my name. She can't take that from me.

Wow. That's my silver lining. I have a car I can live in when my mother inevitably kicks me out.

Because I know, in my heart, that Mom didn't soften up about *the gay issue* and prom. She changed her mind because she didn't want *me* to miss *my* prom. And, based on the increasingly desperate hammering on the bathroom door, I'm about to miss it anyway.

My heart pounding, I step into the shoes Mom dyed to match my dress. I catch my breath, then sweep open the door. Somehow, I end up in a cloud of my mother's hugs. I hold on for so long; I don't want to let go. I know what happens next, and I want this moment—when she still loves me—to linger just a little longer.

These are the arms that taught me to ride a bike, and comforted me when I had nightmares. These are the arms that lifted me up when I fell, and pushed me toward things I wanted but wasn't quite brave enough to grasp on my own. One last time, I gather my strength in her embrace.

Mom pulls away, swiping at her eyes. "You're the most beautiful girl in the world."

"Thank you, Mommy," I say, barely keeping it together myself.

"What a shame John Cho can't see you like this. You deserve to have a date tonight."

Now. I have to do this now before I lose my courage again. I don't want to . . . I can't . . . God, prom is almost here, and I have to do this. The words taste like ash, and I force them out. "Mom, about that. I have to tell you something."

"Not now," she says as she takes my wrist, sweeping me toward the front door. She grabs my clutch and forces it into my hand. There's the slightest hint of annoyance in her voice, but it's fond. "The first part of your surprise showed up early."

For a millisecond, my heart convinces me that she's going to open the salon door and Emma will be standing there. But the thought flits away almost as quickly as it arrived. The cool evening air hits me, and I swear it hisses on my skin.

The girl of my dreams isn't standing there with flowers in her hands.

Instead, waiting at the curb is a limo. A stretch SUV, as a matter of fact. Shelby and Kaylee pop out of the moon roof. Music pours out, and they throw up their arms and squeal when they see me. They're already corsaged, and from the sounds of it, pre-gaming with a hit of secret schnapps.

"Get in, loser, we're going to prom!"

"Mom," I shout, "something's going to happen tonight. You need to know—"

"Don't spoil this," she says, catching my face in her hands. "I've worked very hard on this night, and I want to enjoy it, too. You're going to have a wonderful prom, like a normal girl. I've made sure of that."

"What does that mean?" I ask, but it's too late. She pushes me into the limo's open door. I'm engulfed by a wave of heat and the funk of too much cologne on brand-new leather. It's like being kidnapped by Abercrombie & Fitch.

The door slams closed behind me, and the SUV takes off at top speed. What is happening? *Why* is this happening? I can't even get settled as I strain to look out the back window. The last coherent thought I have as I watch my mother grow smaller and smaller in the distance is:

I didn't even get to tell her I loved her, one last time.

15. On the Steps of the Palace

EMMA

As promised on prom night, there are flowers. And limos. And pictures.

Oh my god, so many pictures that I'm seeing nothing but flashbulb leopard spots. Oh, and the occasional glimpse of the bouquet of tastefully selected orchids, lilies, and roses I clutch in my hands. Their rich perfume goes straight to my head, but that's okay. Everything's been happening so fast today that it's good to have a chance to stop and literally smell the flowers.

Barry sits next to me in the limo, handsome in his tux—it doesn't change colors, I already asked. Next to Dee Dee, he'll be the best-dressed chaperone in the whole county. She's positioned herself closest to the window that separates us from the chauffeur. She talks so fast, he doesn't manage to reply, but that's okay. I think this is how Dee Dee flirts?

Barry, on the other hand, has a quiet serenity to him tonight, which is a whole new side. Clutching the bouquet tighter in my sweaty hands, I ask him, "Nervous?"

"Contemplative," he says. "How are you feeling?"

"Like I swallowed an angry bag of snakes. But I'm going to make you proud."

"Sweetie." Barry turns toward me. "This isn't about me. This is about you, and I promise, you're going to have the time of your life."

I can't even say, *I hope you're right*. Like, it catches in my throat. The bag of snakes gives a good, solid twist, and the only thing that comes out of me is a weird little squeak.

Warmth pours from Barry when he asks, "What's your date wearing?" He's trying to distract me, and I'm going to let him.

"I don't know. Her mother bought it for her, but I haven't seen it."

"What, no fashion show?"

Poor, sweet Barry. He's been out so long, he has no idea what it's like to be in. I can't even imagine that—going a whole day without checking myself. Without looking too long in the wrong direction, without cautiously measuring the things I say. I'm glad it's far behind him, but it makes him seem just a little more out of reach. "I've never been to her house. Her mom doesn't know about us, remember?"

He shakes his head. "How long have you been together?"

"A year and a half," I say. "And before that, it was a year and a half of really clumsy, careful flirting. I knew I was crazy for her the day I met her. But I couldn't just, you know, make a move."

"My heart!"

"She's coming out tonight," I say, and I can't believe I let the words out. I've been holding them so close to my heart, close enough to feel the shimmer of hope but too tightly to really let it grow.

Alyssa's been talking about coming out for a long time now, and there's always a reason why it can't happen. She says tonight, and I believe her. But I didn't want to jinx it by saying it out loud. It feels like tempting fate, but it's too late to worry about that, I guess.

"That's a big deal," Barry says. "If I'd known, I would have baked a cake!"

Instead of laughing, I choke on a sob. All the feelings I've been pushing down come up at once. Everything that's happened in the last couple of weeks, it's like getting hit by different trains, over and over. Joy and fear and hatred and hope and . . . I confess to Barry, "I'm so scared."

"Oh no, honey, we don't cry on prom night. Hey. Come here."

He slides toward me and raises an arm. I slip beneath it and remember all the times I sat like this with my dad—before. When I was little, and still perfect in his eyes. We'd sneak and watch scary movies. When it got to be too much, I'd hide my face against his shoulder and he'd tell me when it was safe to look again. God, I miss my dad, and how can I miss him when he threw me away?

"Talk to your auntie," he says. "What are you scared of? An unfortunate selection of evolutionary dead ends?"

That's good. If I can remember it, I'm going to steal it. I glance up at him and say, "They all hate me. They don't want me to be here tonight."

"Hey, look." And he waits for me to look. I feel like there

should be an orchestra warming up nearby, but he doesn't burst into song. Instead, he chucks my chin and says, "You know what? I didn't go to my own prom, because just like your mystery girlfriend, I was scared out of my Buster Browns."

I have no idea what those are, but I nod.

"But you? You're a queen. When you walk into that gym tonight, you know what your haters are going to see? The bravest person on the planet, and she's going to look fabulous in blue."

"Or pink," I say, trying to joke. "Or green. It *is* a Gregg Barnes original."

"You bet your bottom dollar it is. Emma, honey. You're scared. Fine. Be scared. On the inside. On the outside, be the soft butch you were always meant to be. Life is not a dress rehearsal. You're afraid they're going to look at you? I say, *Good! Look! Take it all in!*"

"I'm not sure—"

Barry presses a finger to my lips. "Shhh. You wanted this. You fought for this. And you're going to walk in there and make it clear that tonight belongs to *you*. This *school* belongs to you."

I start to shake my head, but then I realize: he's right. I fought this fight. I won this battle. I could have walked away—I wanted to so many times. It would have been easier. Looking away is painful, but it's easy. Absorbing hurt instead of pushing back against it—painful, but easy.

Right now, everybody at James Madison High knows my name. They know my power. Broadway literally came to Indiana to stand at my side. I'm not alone. And I'm about to have the night of my life.

"You're right," I finally say.

Barry fans himself with one hand. "My favorite words."

I barely have time to laugh before the limo stops. My snakes turn into butterflies—big, beautiful butterflies soaring and flying and defying gravity. Barry holds me back when I go to open the door. "Oh, girl, you have so much to learn."

Then, when the chauffeur opens the door for us, Dee Dee takes his hand and glides to her feet. She's decked out in gold leopard print, from head to toe, and I think I just heard her purr.

The chauffeur releases her and reaches back for my hand. I take it and haul myself onto the sidewalk as gracefully as I can manage. A breeze whips up my skirt, and I clutch it in a panic.

Behind me, Barry . . . well, he slinks out of the limo. There's no other word for it. He's instant diva, and it's a little disconcerting. He's been so godmothery that it never occurred to me that he might flirt with someone. For real. After an over-appreciative look at the chauffeur, Barry says in a brand-new baritone, "Thank you, darling."

"You're welcome, sir," the chauffeur says, and he looks back! He glances at Barry's face, and then . . . Barry's cummerbund. That was not a hallucination; he totally checked Barry out! The gaybies are blooming in Indiana!

I'm pretty sure I hear Dee Dee mutter, "Bitch," at Barry.

In return, Barry cheerfully murmurs, "Harridan."

Maybe tomorrow, after the ball, I'll ask Barry and Dee Dee if they're actually friends. But that's tomorrow, and I'm gazing in wonder at tonight. Balloons bob from the lampposts, and the lights flooding from the school seem enchanted. There's a glow in the air; the clouds are low, and they reflect the golden brightness beneath them. The sky is like silk, washing in elegant swirls overhead. The air is cold and crisp. It's like a sudden kiss in the dark, and boy howdy, in this dress, I feel it everywhere.

A heavy bassline thumps through the concrete block walls, reverberating all the way out here. I can't make out the song, but I don't care. It's prom night. It's finally here.

"May I?" Barry asks, offering his elbow.

"I'd be delighted," I say, taking it.

We walk up to the school together, Dee Dee outpacing us easily. The front doors are pushed open. I go here every day, but it's different tonight. Bright and buzzy and . . . really weirdly empty. Everyone's probably already in the gym. We're supposed to stay in the gym during dances—no wandering the halls.

Allegedly, some guy named Winston McCarthy discovered the access tunnels under the school and ran an extremely (from what I hear) profitable casino down there. It lasted three whole semesters before he got caught. What a legend. It's a shame he doesn't have a trophy of his own in the Hall of Champions. Instead, he lives on in oral tradition, like all good folk heroes should.

"Where are we meeting your inamorata?" Barry asks.

"Inside," I say. I'm strangling her bouquet. I'm afraid if I loosen my grip I might drop them. I'm about to see her face; we're about to show the world we're in love. Tonight, everything changes. Every step toward the gym feels like a step toward destiny.

We're about to open the doors of the gym when I hear

Principal Hawkins shouting from behind. "Emma! Wait!" He's jogging down the hall toward us.

We turn, and to my horror (and delight, lbr), Barry whistles under his breath at him. I mean, Principal Hawkins looks really distinguished in a tux, so if I were into super old humans and also guys, I might whistle, too. Instead, I smile and call back, "Principal Hawkins!"

Except . . . he's not smiling.

And he's not alone. Nan is doing the scary speed walk she usually reserves for Black Friday sales. Her grim expression sends a wave of fear through me. I clutch Barry's arm a little tighter. "What's going on?"

"I tried to catch you before you left home," Principal Hawkins says when he catches up. He's not breathless; he just sounds broken. "Emma, I'm so sorry."

Alyssa's not coming. Of course she'd be responsible enough to leave a message with a trusted figure of authority. Of course she'd be too afraid to tell me herself. All the snaky butterflies inside me turn to ash. I have a prom, but I don't have a date.

Dee Dee's voice explodes behind us, filling the air. "What have they done?!"

Barry and I turn at the same time. Dee Dee throws herself in front of Nan so she can get to me first. She grabs my shoulders and drags me to her chest. Her comforting pats are like ninja death slices, all up and down my back. She keens, her voice echoing down the hall. "How could they? How *dare* they?"

Pulling myself free, I look at all of them. "How could they what?"

Dee Dee's hesitation is the flicker of an eyelash.

Previously, I've mentioned that I'm not particularly athletic, but when the world grinds to a halt, it turns out I move pretty fast.

I burst past Dee Dee and run into the gym. It's decorated with glittery moons and tinfoil stars overhead, with indigo streamers and flickering white lights. There's a table with punch and cookies, and a photo booth with a box full of props like top hats and boas.

The stage is hung with silver streamers, but the DJ isn't a DJ. It's an iPod in a Bluetooth dock, blasting out somebody's personal prom playlist. The floor is empty. The seats are empty. The gym is empty.

I've never wanted more to faint in my life than I do right now. But I'm not that girl, apparently. I'm the girl who keeps on standing, no matter how hard you hit her. I absorb those blows. I take those hits. The flowers slip from my hand, dropping to the glossy hardwood with a plaintive sigh.

The adults press in behind me. I hear their voices; I feel their presence. But it doesn't matter what they're saying. I thought I had imagined the worst possible scenario: that Alyssa wouldn't show. I'd even prepared for it, a tiny little bit.

But this.

Who could have imagined anything like this?

"Pictures started showing up on social media about a half an hour ago," Principal Hawkins says, from far, far away. "And I have a text from the PTA. They say they did their due diligence. They threw an inclusive prom for Emma. It's not their fault if their children chose to attend a private dance at the Elks Club instead."

He said the message came from the PTA. But the PTA can't text; it's an organization, like the Klan or the Kardashians. No. That text came from Mrs. Greene, and that means she plotted this. Planned it. Executed it like a crime boss.

But I don't understand, because I have texts from Alyssa. She's been texting me, like, all day. Talking about her crazy mom, and last-minute crazy, and crazycrazycrazy. Texts that stopped . . . about an hour ago.

They planned this. Mrs. Greene planned this. Shelby and Kaylee and Nick and Kevin and everybody else in school *planned* this!

Flattened, Barry says, "I think I'm going to cry. They went behind her back? The whole *town* kept this from her?"

"How could they do this to us?" Dee Dee wails. "This was supposed to be an easy win! God, somebody wake me from this PR nightmare!"

Nan rounds on Dee Dee. "Excuse me, easy win?"

Principal Hawkins turns on her, too. "Wait. Is that why you came here? For the publicity?"

I look to Barry. Barry in his tux. Barry who brought me dresses I didn't even want. Auntie Barry, Barry who swears he knows just what this is like. Sympathetic, sweet-talking Barry.

Numb, I say, "I'm just a publicity stunt for you?"

"This is what we're going to do," Barry says, ignoring my question. His face is pink, and his brow is starting to shine. "We're getting right back in that limo, and we're going to that other prom, and we are going to—"

"Stop it! Just stop!"

I shout it above the noise of the iPod DJ, above the sound

of Barry's and Dee Dee's egos. This was never about me. Not for them. Principal Hawkins was just thrilled I wasn't on meth. Nan fought the fight because I asked her to; I guess I never asked if she thought I *should*. And Alyssa . . . no. I can't even think her name right now.

Barry reaches out. "Emma . . ."

I shove his hand away. "I don't want any more help, okay? Go ahead and go to the other prom, Mr. Pecker. I'm sure you'll have no trouble getting in!"

And then I walk away. I don't even try to run. I walk, with my big dinosaur bones, and my big monster feet, in this stupid monster dress I never wanted to wear, right out of James Madison High.

Maybe for good.

16. The Nicest Kids in Town

ALYSSA

"Where are we?" I ask when the limo stops.

I have to ask that, because this isn't James Madison, therefore, this can't be prom. My thoughts spin like mad, trying to make sense of this.

Mom said something about *one* of my surprises. I assumed that a ride with people who haven't really been my friends since third grade was enough surprise to last a lifetime. But no, now we're at an undisclosed location.

Nobody answers me. Instead, Kaylee holds out her phone and goes cheek to cheek with Shelby. They hold up peace signs, trying to look as cute as possible before the flash goes off, and then Kaylee instantly pulls up the snap. Present-moment Kaylee smiles at digital, two-seconds-ago Kaylee.

"I hate to sound conceited," Kaylee says disingenuously, "but even I would do me."

"I'd do you, too," Shelby chimes in. Then she instantly amends, "No homo."

It will come as no surprise if I tell you that Nick and Kevin agree with all levels of hotness proposed by the girls who were very recently semi-permanent residents of their laps.

The guys spill out of the limo, leaving the three of us to see ourselves out. Once we do, it's pretty clear we're all glowing under the light of the Elks Club sign.

All around us, people stream toward the doors. Each time they open, a blast of music escapes. Laughter drifts around us, excited squeals punctuated by the bright pop of phones on selfie sticks.

I put a hand out, holding Kaylee back on the sidewalk. "I'm not kidding, what's going on?"

"Look," Kaylee says, her voice a cauldron of pure, unadulterated nasty-nice, "realize that we're doing you a favor and say thank you, Alyssa."

"It's okay that you don't care about being popular, but we're saving you from yourself." Shelby nods, and her dangling earrings swing like pendulums. They catch the light: bright, then dark, almost hypnotic.

Leaning in, Kaylee whispers, "We know about you and Emma."

Her words punch through me, knocking the breath from my lungs.

"You don't want to be a messiah," Shelby adds.

Jaw dropped, I hear myself correcting Shelby instead of processing what they've just said. "You mean *pariah*."

Cheerfully, Shelby links arms with Kaylee and shrugs. "Whatever. It's prom. It's our night. Let's go and have fun!"

"No, wait," I say sharply, staying them with a hand. "What do you mean you know?"

Kaylee rolls her eyes. Her thick, spider-leg lashes flutter as she shakes her head. "Anna Kendrick and John Cho? Two mysterious dates from other schools, one for the town lesbo and one for the student council president who thinks she's subtle when she holds her hand in public? I mean, come on."

"Plus, you're always standing up for her," Shelby notes casually. "And you let those weirdos from New York come to our meeting. It's kind of obvious."

"Why didn't you say anything?" I ask, feeling faint and slightly sick.

Annoyed, Kaylee chooses her words carefully and speaks them very slowly. "Because we didn't want your mom to cancel prom, dummy."

"Yay prom!" Shelby says, throwing a victory hand to the sky. "Come on, it's starting, let's go!"

Cocooned in a numb haze, I go along as Kaylee and Shelby manage to hustle me inside. All this time with Emma, I've been careful; we've been *so* careful. Kaylee and Shelby aren't idiots, but they're the most self-absorbed people I know—and *they* caught on? My heart slips between beats and my ears ring as we walk inside.

Red and gold cover everything. Cardboard genie lamps hang from the ceiling. Big loops of red gauze ring the tables. Little paper camels scatter across the refreshment table. They graze among gold plastic cups and red paper plates, next to a massive plastic bowl full of jewel-red punch. Even the picture station is a vaguely Middle Eastern tent with a banner over it that says: 1,001 NIGHTS.

I'm mortified, especially when I see some of the basketball

team wearing turbans. This is not the prom we've been planning since Christmas. This is some racist monstrosity, pulled from an alternate universe.

And Emma is nowhere to be found. I reach for my phone and realize that I don't have it. It's still on Joan's station at the salon. Kaylee and Shelby peeled away as soon as we hit the door, which leaves me alone to search for Emma.

It feels like a funhouse in here, red lights pulsing across familiar faces, the shadows distorting them. The laughter is too loud, and it vibrates on a frequency that goes straight down my spine. No one's touching me, but I feel pushed and pulled and shoved, fighting through the haze of a smoke machine and the sharp daggers of lights that flash on the floor.

I search everywhere: the dance floor, the bathrooms, even the kitchenette, where PTA moms are shoveling sherbert into a backup punch bowl at breakneck speed.

Breathless and panicked, I duck back into the main room. Leaning against the wall for support, I squint and stare, scanning the crowd over and over, hoping to see one face, *that* face.

None of this makes sense. This time yesterday, I was still helping set up the gym for A Night to Remember. My mother mentioned nothing about a change of venue; she was way more interested in waterproof tablecloths and signing off on the DJ's playlist. I don't understand when all of this could have happened.

Somehow, over the roar of the crowd, I hear my mother's voice behind me. She must have gone in the side door and straight to the kitchen. When I turn to walk back inside, she fills the door. The worst, most devastating thing is, she looks *happy*. Like, genuinely happy, in a way I haven't seen since before Dad left.

"What do you think?" she asks, waving a hand at the Arabian Nights around us.

"I think I'm confused, Mother," I say. "Why did you move prom? *When* did you move it?"

"At the last minute. There was a problem that had to be dealt with."

Well, no wonder she's been on her phone all day. I'm afraid to ask when she started planning this move and how apparently everybody knew but me. Was it this morning? Last night? Suddenly, heavy lead melts into my feet, pulling me down. I feel so weighted that I could drop right through the floor. Did she decide to do this the night of the public meeting? When I pushed? *Because* I pushed?

Wait.

I look around again, and a needle of ice threads through my heart. New place, secret location, a problem to be dealt with. It's agonizing to take a breath, but I have to. I have to open my mouth, and I have to ask.

"Mom, where's Emma Nolan?"

My mother laughs lightly, without a hint of steel beneath it. "I'm quite sure she's at her inclusive prom, Alyssa."

"Mom, you didn't . . ."

"I don't like it when strangers presume to come to our community and tell us how to live. Our rules were a problem? Fine, fixing little problems is what I do. And now everyone is happy. She has a prom, and we have our prom."

Stunned, I don't know what to say. I had no idea my mother

could be this cruel. Smoothing her hands down my arms, Mom looks me over again, her smile widening until it's almost maniacal. "I wasn't going to let you miss a night like this, Alyssa. This is for you. I did this all for you."

"This is not—"

She interrupts me. "Now, you go have fun. I'll be here to make sure everything is perfect."

I back away from her, because I don't know this woman. This calculating, manipulative person masquerading as my mother is terrifying. She stepped right out of *Game of Thrones* and into *Game of Proms*. And she won.

I have to get away from Elena Lannister Greene. If I look at her for one more second, I'm honestly afraid I might throw up.

When I whip around, I stumble onto the dance floor, into the throng. Since I can't turn back, I have to wade through a sea of people having the times of their lives. Bodies crash all around me. The music, the voices, they fill my head until they beat against my eardrums to get out. Everything swirls and melts together like a nightmare; I wish I could wake up. I'm not even sure where I'm going—all I know is *away, away*.

Kaylee grabs my arm and jolts me back to the present. "We need to get our picture taken together."

"No. I can't. I have to go—"

"You're part of the prom court, Alyssa. Don't make me get ugly."

My mother really has arranged everything. I can't get away. I can't call for help. I can't even warn Emma. The urge to vomit lurches back up. I clap a hand over my mouth, just in case, and that's all Kaylee needs to drag me off balance and over to the photo booth. The photographer crams me in the middle, with the couples on either side.

She tells them to smile, they say cheese, and a single tear streaks down my cheek.

17. Step Out of the Sun

EMMA

The good thing about your entire life imploding is that people stop questioning your poor choices. I've worn the same pair of pajamas for two days now, and I'm on a strict diet of melted ice cream and chocolate Teddy Grahams.

Today was supposed to be my first day back at school since . . . well, you know. When Nan looked in on me this morning, I didn't even move from my perfect, lumpen position in bed.

"I'm not going," I said.

She closed the door quietly and said nothing.

I know that Barry and Dee Dee have been at the house. It's impossible to miss the reaching-for-the-back-row quality of their voices. Thankfully, Nan keeps sending them away. It saves me the trouble of getting out of bed to find heavy objects to chuck at them.

When I got home from prom, I posted a one-minute video on Emma Sings because I knew people would ask how it went. Then I called Alyssa four thousand times and left four thousand voice mails, in between googling Dee Dee Allen and Barry Glickman. Guess what I found out!

No, don't guess. I'll tell you.

Right before they showed up in Indiana, their new musical bombed. It bombed hard. It bombed so hard, even people in New Jersey hated it. I don't know how long a play is supposed to be on Broadway, but I'm guessing that closing after one night is *bad*.

So, their careers took a header and they picked me as the poster child for their image-rehabilitation tour. Like, they did *interviews* about it—they did a photo shoot with the picket signs before they even left for Indiana.

In a way, I'm not surprised that Dee Dee wanted to use me. Honestly, I wouldn't be surprised if she ate little baby harp seals for breakfast and washed them down with melted polar-ice-cap water—zazz!—but Barry's betrayal exposed a nerve.

I can't believe how stupidly, how easily I trusted him. I can't believe I didn't realize that none of that was for me. Or even *about* me. How could I have been so naive?

Oh, did Alyssa ever call back? Glad you asked, friend. She did not. But there *are* pictures of her reigning in the shadow prom court with Kaylee and Shelby. They all have tiaras, isn't that cute?

Because I'm all about the pain, I scrolled through the #jmprom19 tag for a while. Real prom looked like it was banging, one of those clubs with the velvet rope and very selective guest list. Picture after picture, I studied the details. Memorized the faces. Made a mental inventory with a neat little tab at the top: enemies.

And picture after picture, I searched for signs of Alyssa in them. I only found a couple, mostly with the gruesome two-some. But! There was one super adorable mommy-daughter picture from the photo booth.

Mrs. Greene was auditioning to play the Joker in hers, her lips a slash of scarlet lipstick and her mouth full of hundreds of big white teeth. Alyssa's smile was more pained, but it was there.

Yep. She still had a smile left in her. At the absolute worst moment of my high school career, my girlfriend smiled for the official photographer of James Madison High's actual real prom for actually real people.

I tortured myself with that for a while, screenshotting the pictures and arranging them in their own album. Back and forth, just looking at Alyssa. Analyzing her face. I mean, I've been studying it for years, and I can tell she's not having the time of her life. But I can also tell that she's at the *secret prom she didn't tell me about.*

After a while, I turned off my phone and threw it at the pile of laundry in the corner of my room. And there it remains. Hence the Nan alarm clock and the engulfing silence in my room. It's good. It gives me a chance to sleep. Sleep and I go way back; a growing girl totally needs eighteen or more hours a day of un-consciousness, right? Bring on the dreamless dark; I'll just Rip Van Winkle my way through graduation and summer break.

Except, I've slept so much the past couple of days that my back kind of aches, and I'm not tired at all. Instead, all the squirrels in my brain got into some caffeine, and my mind lurches from dead stop to top speed.

It kicks in with all the things I've been trying not to consider, like what the hell is wrong with me that this stuff keeps happening? Was I a serial killer in my past life and that's why this one sucks? Am I atoning for metaphysical mistakes? Or am I just cursed in this one? Maybe I ate some witch's radishes and cabbages when I was a toddler.

This is stupid.

I roll out of bed and onto my feet. If I'm going to hate myself, my life, and everyone in it, I'm gonna need more ice cream. Pulling a robe over my pajamas, I studiously ignore the mirror. Y'all, I'm experiencing the sensation of my hair sticking up in a giant wing on one side and being matted flat on the other. I don't need visual confirmation.

My palms itch as I pass the pile of clothes where I threw my phone. My brain tells me to keep walking, there's Rocky Road waiting in the kitchen. But my stupid, stupid heart wants to see if Alyssa ever replied. I stare at the pile for a second, debating what to do, but I already know what I'm going to do.

I plunge my hand into a tangle of inside-out jeans and snatch my phone; I'm a bear in a salmon stream. First try, and I got it. A wide streak of nausea breaks through the numbness as I wait for my phone to turn back on.

When it finally boots, it makes one chirpy text sound, and then it blows up. Text notifications scroll like it's the latest Star Wars movie. YouTube sent me a ton of notifications, too. Oh, and voice mails—eight of those.

Before I can start my deep dive, the phone rings. I yelp in surprise and almost throw it across the room. The ID flashes on the screen. Alyssa. Just seeing her name is a punch in the gut, and I consider rejecting the call. But my stupid, stupid thumb touches the green icon and I say, "Hello?"

"Emma," Alyssa says. Her voice is hoarse; it sounds like she might have been crying. "Are you there?"

Sinking into my laundry pile, I struggle to speak. Finally, I manage, "Yeah, it's me."

"Oh my god, are you all right??"

I laugh. Seriously, I laugh. Is that a real question? "No, I'm great. I'm fantastic. I mean, sure, my girlfriend went to a secret prom with people she swears she can't stand and left me hanging at A Ghost Town to Remember by myself, but it's fine. It's all fine. I'm *so* fine."

"I'm so sorry, Emma," Alyssa warbles. "I swear, I had no idea."

Oh good. Anger just showed up to the party. I like anger. It's nice and clean and specific. "How could you not know? Your mother was the host; you were on prom committee!"

With a sniffle, Alyssa says, "They hid it from me. And then Kaylee and Shelby dropped a bomb on me. They figured out that we're together, and they wanted to make sure prom happened. The whole PTA was planning behind my back."

"I don't believe you."

Shock crackles on the line. "Do you really think I would do something like this to you?"

"I don't think," I shout. "It happened. I saw the pictures. Nice tiara, by the way."

Alyssa pleads, but it's laced with irritation. "What is it going to take to prove it to you? Because I didn't know. My mother stalked me the whole night. I didn't have my phone, and I couldn't sneak out, and I'm so, so sorry, Emma, but I didn't know they were going to do this to you. I've been shaking and crying for two days."

"Well, that makes two of us."

"Please, Emma. Please."

"Fine," I say, because this hurts. It feels like an axe to the chest, splitting me right down the middle. Hearing Alyssa cry makes me want to comfort her. But knowing why she's crying makes me want to scream. "Come see me. Tell me face-to-face, so I can look in your eyes."

"I can't."

Ha. I ask for one thing, and it's already a no. Thumping my head back against the wall, I ask, "You can't, or you won't?"

Lowering her voice, Alyssa says, "My mom is here. I think she knows, and she's doing everything she can to *not* know. She's watching me every second."

Everything she just said is a slap in the face. All of this fighting, all of this negotiating for months about prom, and whether we'd go together, whether we'd tell people, and . . . she thinks her mom already knows? I can't hide my frustration. If my hair weren't so greasy, I'd pull it.

"Oh my god, Alyssa, if you think she knows, just tell her! Tell her we're in love! That was the plan, right?"

"I can't," she says, plaintive and small. "It's bad enough that Kaylee and Shelby know."

Oh. Oh wow. My anger keys up to white hot, so hot I barely feel it anymore. I have so much heat, I could punch through the atmosphere. I could boil oceans and scorch the earth.

She's been using her mom as the reason she can't come out

for months, and suddenly I realize, it's not a reason. It's an *excuse*. Yeah, her mom is obviously a bigot and a homophobe, but it looks like Alyssa's carrying some of that on her own.

Slowly, I repeat, "*Bad* enough?"

"That's not what I mean."

"And yet, that's exactly what you said," I snap.

"Emma, I'm sorry."

What is she apologizing for, exactly? The wrong words? Or for the way she really feels about us? It doesn't matter. I'm out of bandwidth. I can't fake cheerful, but bitter works. "Okay, great. That fixes everything. Thanks for calling!"

Then I hang up. I hang up on Alyssa Greene, the girl at the church picnic, my first love, my first kiss, my first everything. So true, on so many levels, because she was my first real secret, too. She was the longest lie I ever told. I wanted her to be happy; I didn't want her to lose everything like I did.

We're so freaking close to college. She's so close to being free from her mom and her mom's neuroses, and I thought, I really thought that this time, she'd come out and we'd be together, for real, no more hiding.

But all this time, I thought her mom was the only thing holding her back. Her family. Truly, I believed that until fifteen seconds ago when she said it was *bad enough* that Kaylee and Shelby knew.

Now Alyssa Greene's my first heartbreak, and I think I'm going to die of it.

18. Five Hundred Twenty-Five Thousand Six Hundred Minutes

ALYSSA

I have watched the video Emma put up on prom night a thousand times.

"This is how it went," Emma tells the camera, combing her fingers through her hair. There are still hints of makeup on her face, but she's already changed into a T-shirt. Specifically, a T-shirt that reads: BEHOLD THE FIELD IN WHICH I GROW MY F*CKS, LAY THINE EYES UPON IT AND SEE THAT IT IS BARREN.

Adjusting the laptop screen, she gazes down into its glow. "Well, it didn't. I mean, yeah, the gym was decorated and there was music playing, but I was the only one there. It turns out, I was the only one who wanted to go to the inclusive prom. Everybody else, including—no, let's just say everybody else—went to the secret, *not*-inclusive prom. But hey, at least I got to take all these cool pictures for my Insta story!"

And then there's this brief, awful slideshow that she set to the sad angel song from the dog commercial—pictures of the gym, empty. Of the chairs and tables, empty. Of the stage, empty. Of party favors and punch bowls untouched. The screen goes black, and this glittery font swirls across the screen: *Happy Prom Night!*

It's short, and Emma's wrecked. I keep watching it because I'm hoping that . . . I don't know. That the past will change? That the hurt will fade? That somehow it might end differently? I don't know what I hope, but I hate that I see her heart break in real time.

But I'm glad she didn't come to school today. Everybody's talking about her video, and it's really weird. Some people are mad she won't drop the issue; others have started to feel guilty. But all of them are obsessed with the number of views she's getting and the semi-famous people who've shared the link— I'm pretty sure anyone who's written a young adult novel in the last three years has tweeted about it, as have tons of Broadway people . . . and plenty of journalists.

Which is why Principal Hawkins completely changed our end-of-day routine. We're not allowed to go out the front doors like usual. We're exiting directly into the student parking lot through the gym doors and going straight to our cars or buses.

A fleet of reporters showed up just after lunch and set up in the front lot. They have cameras and glossy-haired reporters with microphones, and we've been told explicitly that we're not allowed to talk to any of them without a parent present.

Breanna Lo touches me on the shoulder. When I turn around, she's holding up her iPhone. "I'm doing an episode of my podcast about the promtroversy, can I get a quote?"

"It was unkind and unfair, and it never should have been an issue to begin with."

"Love it," Breanna says. She scrolls on her screen, then asks,

"And just for the record, we're speaking to Alyssa Greene, our student council president. Alyssa, can you tell us which prom you attended?"

My tongue fills my mouth, and I shake my head. I should have listened to Principal Hawkins—no talking to reporters of any kind.

With as much grace as I can manage, I bail on Breanna and duck outside to get to my car. Even though we're not supposed to be filmed, plenty of people are dragging themselves past the cameras, just casually making sure they'll be seen.

Mr. Thu comes out and starts to hurry people along, but there's only so much narcissism he can tamp down on his own. I try to keep my head lowered as I pull out of the school lot. But as I turn toward home, I catch a glimpse of a car that looks just like—no, it *is* my mother's.

Craning around, I'm shattered with cold when I see her standing in the field across from the school, holding her coat closed and talking to a news crew from Indianapolis. Oh god, what is she saying now? Why can't she just leave this alone?

I look back at the road just in time to slam on my brakes. My whole body stiffens, and the shock pushes the breath out of my lugs. I almost hit the car in front of me. An accident, right in front of James Madison, is the last thing I need right now.

Traffic crawls into town. This is ridiculous; I'm going four miles an hour. At this rate, I'll get home next Thursday. I throw on my turn signal and pull into the Walmart parking lot. I don't need anything, but it's a good place to hang out. There are tables out front, and the Coke machines are cheap.

When I pull in, it's obvious I'm not the only person who had this idea. A bunch of the guys from the basketball team are slow-rolling their pickups past the entrance, leaning out of windows to holler at the girls at the table. It's what this place looks like on a Friday night, except it's full daylight and we're all in our school clothes.

"Heyyy, Alyssa," Shelby calls as I walk up.

Kaylee gives me a little finger wave. "Come sit, queen."

Inside, I feel hesitation, but my legs carry me right over. I don't want to sit with them. I don't even want to look at them, and yet somehow, my mother has reengineered my life. I'm back in elementary school, when she picked my clothes and my friends and dictated everything about my day. I'm a leaf in the wind, helpless to choose my direction, at the mercy of outside forces.

"Did you know our school is on CNN?" Kaylee says, turning to let one of her sub-minions braid her hair.

"What?" I say flatly.

"Yeah, the home page." She makes a sour face, then quotes the headline. "'Edgewater, Indiana, overflows with bigotry.' Like, seriously? They're acting like we're monsters."

Shelby bobs her head like a good hench-cheerleader. "Seriously. We gave her a prom, god."

I start to say something—I'm not even sure what—but there's a quiet roar that runs through the people collected on the tables. Suddenly, someone shouts, "It's Mr. Pecker!"

We all crane our necks, and then more people call out. It's a hailstorm of *Pecker!*s, and I can't believe that Mr. Glickman is walking out of the Walmart with a little bag clutched in his hands. I didn't realize he was still in town; I assumed he and Ms. Allen packed up after prom night and headed back to New York City.

"Say it!" Shelby yells, cupping her hands around her mouth to amplify it.

Nick and Kevin bound out of the bed of a pickup to join us, and they chant it, too. "Say it! Say it!"

Mr. Glickman takes a deep breath and rolls his eyes. Without much enthusiasm, he spits out Mr. Pecker's signature phrase from *Talk to the Hand*. "It's Pecker time."

Everybody roars and cheers. Kaylee nudges Shelby, pressing quarters into her hand. "Can we get you something to drink, Mr. Pecker?"

He wraps a hand around his throat. "This . . . is a finely tuned instrument. I will not insult it with"—he takes a look at the cans on the table—"Diet Mountain Lightning."

Nostrils curling, Kaylee rolls a shoulder. "Fine, then."

Mr. Glickman takes a few steps like he's leaving. Then he spins on his toe, coming back around to face us. It looks kind of practiced, but to be fair, everything Ms. Allen and Mr. Glickman do looks rehearsed. "You know, I think I've been unfair. Coming to your charming little hamlet, making demands."

"You made my mom cry rage tears," Shelby volunteers.

Mr. Glickman puts a hand to his chest. "Oh no, did I? How?"

Shelby waves a hand around, "You know. Trying to make our prom all gay."

"I see, I see, I see," Mr. Glickman says. He doesn't catch my eye—he probably doesn't even remember who I am. But his gaze seems to slide past me. Which is good, because I was right—this isn't entirely spontaneous.

I have a feeling he's about to make an argument he's made before—a performance pretending to be a conversation. This is exactly the way I talk to people who want the student council to make 4/20 a school holiday, or Domino's the official sponsor of our cafeteria.

Kaylee leans back on the table and eyes him. "So, are you sorry?"

"Exquisitely apologetic," Mr. Glickman says. "Do you object to me?"

"Nah," Nick says with a laugh. "You're Mr. Pecker!"

"Then could one of you darling little urchins explain to me why you didn't want Emma at your prom?"

"Because, you know, it's wrong." Kevin says this like it's the most obvious answer in the world. Then, to bolster his case, he says, "It's in the Bible."

"And we believe in the Bible." Shelby nods and nestles down beneath Kevin's arm. Kevin stretches out his arm around Shelby's back and subtly tugs on the cup of her bra. She giggles but doesn't shoo him away. Charming.

Mr. Glickman surveys them slowly. "I see. It's in the Bible, and you're true believers. If that's the case, aren't you afraid?"

"Of what?" Nick asks.

Ohhhh yeah. Here we go. I see where this is going now, and it surprises me that they don't. Well, no, I guess it doesn't surprise me.

We all have Bibles with white leather covers, presents for graduating from Sunday school to Youth Celebration! But we're not exactly encouraged to read from beginning to end.

We have discussion guides that focus on certain stories, that tell us how we should feel and think about said certain stories. Usually, they're parables and miracles, occasionally inspirational women or acts of faith. It's not a deep dive by any stretch of the imagination.

Gracefully, Mr. Glickman slides to sit on the bench. With a wave of his hand, he gestures at Kaylee's foot. "Well, I see that this lovely young woman has a charming dolphin tattoo on her ankle."

Kaylee warms back up, now that the topic of conversation has turned back to her favorite subject. "Spring break, last year. The guy said I had the best ankles he'd ever inked."

"I bet he did," Mr. Glickman says agreeably. "Too bad you're going to Hell for it."

"Excuse me?" Kaylee yelps.

"Well, it's in the Bible."

Setting her face in a scowl, Kaylee says, "No it's not."

"'Ye shall not print any marks upon you,'" Mr. Glickman says. "Look it up, it's in Leviticus."

Kaylee whips out her phone. She doesn't even have to google it; she has a Bible app right there on the home screen. It's visible the very second she finds the passage in question. Some of the fire goes out of her—more because she's wrong than because she's really worried about going to Hell, would be my guess. She slaps her phone facedown and says, "That doesn't count."

"So, you can pick and choose?" Mr. Glickman asks. He doesn't let her answer, though. He rolls his head to look at

Kevin. "Because let me guess, sir. You see plenty of action."

"I get mine," Kevin says, pulling on his varsity jacket, and Shelby giggles against him again.

"Well, then that means everyone at your church gets to throw rocks at your precious, precious head until you *die*."

Shelby looks distressed. "Noooooooo. Not my Kevin's head!"

"There's no way that's in the Bible," Kevin says, because he obviously didn't learn his lesson from Kaylee looking up a verse not two seconds ago. And, since she's not about to be the only one who gets shamed this day, she helpfully does just that.

Flashing her phone at Kevin and Shelby, Kaylee says, "Ope, sorry, guys. You're getting stoned, and not the fun way."

With a snort, Nick points at Shelby and Kevin. And then, out loud, he literally says, "Ha ha!"

"Don't think you're out of the woods, young man," Mr. Glickman tells Nick. "If I'm not mistaken, that's a polyester jacket and those are denim blue jeans. To Hell with you for wearing two kinds of cloth!"

I press my lips together and watch as they look it up, as everyone else around us starts to murmur.

"Who loves beefy nachos supreme?" Mr. Glickman asks, and then announces gleefully at the hands that go up, "Hell for you, and you, and you! Don't you know the Bible says you can't mix meat and milk in the same meal?"

The murmurs grow a little louder. Other people have pulled out their phones to fact-check this. They skim through, and I hear pop-up whispers around me. Milo from the FCK curses under his breath because he found a rule about planting two kinds of crops in one field; someone else is baffled by *tearing your clothes*. This is probably the closest any of us have read the Bible in our lives . . . and I think it might be working?

"This is a lot of rules," Shelby says quietly.

Kevin adds, "I didn't know any of this was in here."

While I marvel at the sudden change at the table, Mr. Glickman stands up, smoothing hands down the front of his suit. "There's one more thing in there you should look at. You should know that I have played Jesus Christ on three separate occasions, in *Superstar*, in *Godspell*, and in my shiksa aunt Dorothy's living nativity. And do you know what I've taken away from it?"

Since no one else says it, I volunteer. "What, Mr. Glickman?"

"First, it takes a Jew to play the messiah with authority," he says, gesturing at himself extravagantly. "And second, when asked which law was the most important, the man himself said that *love thy neighbor* was the only rule he cared about."

Fingers fly across screens, now searching for that phrase. Heads bob all around, and eyes raise to Mr. Glickman. Fighting back a smile, I watch as he plays my classmates like fiddles.

He says, gently, "And if you ask me, I don't think anybody showed Miss Emma much love on prom night."

Kaylee frowns. "Stop trying to get into our heads."

"I mean," Shelby says, "he's not wrong. We used to hang out with her."

"Before she turned gay!"

"If she turned, that implies she had no choice." Mr. Glickman shrugs expansively, as if to say, *I don't make the rules.*

"And if she had no choice, doesn't that mean God made her that way?"

"That's not how it works."

Mr. Glickman turns his gaze to Shelby. "Oh no? When did you choose to be straight?"

"Never," Shelby says. "I just am."

Mr. Glickman is silent for a minute, watching Shelby's face until understanding finally dawns on her. With a little bow of his head, Mr. Glickman spreads his hands. His point is made. Then he stands up and gathers his purchases. The thin plastic of the bag reveals a box of Throat Coat tea and a *People* magazine.

"I must be off," Mr. Glickman says warmly. "But say it with me, once more?"

And then the Walmart parking lot fills with dozens of voices, all crying out at once:

"It's Pecker time!"

19. Their Voices Soft as Thunder

EMMA

When I emerge from my misery cocoon with my laptop, Nan scrambles to turn off the television.

"Subtle," I say as I sit beside her on the couch. Pushing the screen back so she can see, I tell her, "I know it's on the news."

In fact, that's why I came out at all. I finally decided to look at the comments on my prom night video and found that my story went viral. Or at least, the version of the story people can piece together from my video and all the interviews outside the school went viral. Shockingly, except for angry tweets that night, Barry and Dee Dee have been silent.

Nan puts an arm around me and rests her chin on my shoulder. "I'm sorry you have to bear all this, Emma."

Leaning into her, I say, "Yeah, me too. It sucks. And it's not just me, you know? Listen to some of these comments."

I load my channel again, hitting pause on the video. It's not like I need to hear myself explain what happened on prom night again. Instead, I scroll to the comments—and yeah, there are some jerkwads and douche canoes dropping their turds of wisdom. But most of the responses are from kids like me. All over Indiana and the Midwest. Hell, all over the country.

Safe beneath the curve of my grandmother's arm, I start to read. "This girl's from Muncie. She says she was allowed to take her girlfriend to the prom, but they kicked her out because she wore a tux. And this transboy from Seymour actually got the most votes for prom king, but the school wouldn't give it to him. There are, like, six comments from people who said their teachers refuse to use their proper pronouns. Here's a bisexual girl in South Bend who got suspended for wearing a rainbow-flag pin. Nan, it's everywhere. They hate us everywhere."

With a soft sigh, Nan hugs me to her side. "Some of them are scared. And some are ignorant. And yes, some of them are full of hate. We can do something about the first two-thirds, and the ones left over, we leave to God to sort out."

An overwhelming wave of despair crashes over me. Is this going to be my whole life? Constantly explaining myself to the ignorant, always trying to convince people that I'm about as scary as rice pudding, and learning to run and hide from the ones with teeth and claws? This is my forever? I'm suddenly exhausted again.

We're told to hide this beautiful part of ourselves, the falling-in-love part, the dizzy infatuation part. Don't hold hands in your Uber; don't kiss at the movies. Think hard about whether you want to correct a stranger when they ask about your significant other and get the gender wrong. Carefully consider everything you say so these strangers don't spit on you—or worse.

Nan is the one person in my life who can almost read my mind. She shakes me and leans around to make me look in her eyes. "I won't tell you this isn't a trial. But I will tell you this is not the end."

I start to cry. Nan sets my laptop aside so she can wrap both her arms around me. And I just bawl, because the numbness has faded and everything that's left is agony. I don't want to be a news story; I don't want to be a cause. All I wanted was a dance. One night. Barely anything, and I couldn't even have that.

Somewhere, in this same town, my parents are probably watching the news. And they're probably *happy*. Oh, they might pretend to feel bad for me, but it would be in their twisted way. *What a terrible way for Emma to learn the wages of her sin. Maybe this will make her change her mind and her behavior. Maybe she'll repent and we can welcome her home.*

I swear, I didn't come out of my room to cry. I wanted to share the comments on my video. If Nan hadn't seen it, I wanted to show her the terrible things Mrs. Greene told Channel 13 in Indianapolis. Awful, just like the new rules were awful, because people like her have learned to use our words against us. They don't come right out and call us *fag*. Instead, they say things like:

"What happened here was not the result of an elaborate plan to humiliate this girl, as has been reported in the press. The James Madison High PTA felt that Emma would not be safe unless we offered the option of a separate prom for students and parents who objected. Unfortunately, there are people in our community who are offended by her lifestyle, and we felt this arrangement, while not ideal, was the only course of action available to us."

Leaving out the part that she's one of the people in the community, and that she couldn't care less if I'm safe or not. Totally ignoring the part where she's the one who stirred everyone up to begin with.

But it sounds good, doesn't it? It sounds *reasonable*. It sounds so much better than the truth. And it looks like, as long as people learn to lie the right way, they can get away with murder.

My sobs fade after a while, but my chest still hurts. With every single breath, I ache.

Nan proves her love for me once more by mopping up my slick, snotty face with a handful of napkins. Her touch is gentle, her palms warm. She takes my face in her hands and strokes my now-dry cheeks with her thumbs.

She had no idea this is where she would be in her old age, I'm sure. Raising me instead of tearing it up on the riverboat casinos in Rising Sun. Or, I don't know, spending winter in Florida, teaching snowbirds to play euchre so she could whip them at it. Instead, she's stuck here with me. Looking at her, I feel the urge to cry come back up again. I've made everything so hard on her.

"I'm sorry I dragged you into this," I tell her.

Nan takes a deep breath and strokes her fingers through my hair. "Emma, do you remember your great-uncle Donnie?"

The name is vaguely familiar, but I shake my head.

"Well, double great to you. He was my uncle," she says. "He served in the Pacific during World War Two, met his lifelong beau there. Of course, that's not how he introduced him. Frank was his *friend*.

"They went off to live in California, far away from us, to hide their lives. And even though they came to every Thanksgiving and Christmas, even though we ended up calling him Uncle Frank, everybody pretended they were just war buddies. They were together forty-seven years when Uncle Frank passed, and even then, Uncle Donnie never said it out loud.

"They'd been together a quarter of a century before the first pride parade ever happened. They both passed before marriage equality. And I'm telling you this because what you're going through now is terrible. Inexcusable. There are people around here I'd set on fire if I had the chance, and people I wouldn't walk across the street to spit on if they *were* on fire.

"So. If you want to go when you graduate, to New York or San Francisco, I'll do what I can to get you there. I know you planned to go to IU in the fall, but if you want to take a year and settle yourself somewhere more accepting, I won't blame you one bit. I've got some money saved up, even.

"I just want you to know that you are the dream that Uncle Donnie never dared to dream.

"You're seventeen years old; you know who you are. The world knows who you are. It might not mean much to you now. But believe your nan when she tells you that your fight, right here, right now, matters."

My breath shudders as I lean back against her. I had no idea I had a gay uncle and . . . well, that's a problem right there, isn't it? Wrapping Nan's arms around me more tightly, I say, "I'd like to think it does, but I just don't know anymore."

"That's all right, baby," she says. "You don't have to be sure right now. And we can always come back to this later."

"That would be nice, actually." I really mean that, too. There's been way too much talking lately, and too many people talking *for* me, too. Some quiet, inside my head and outside of it, would be a good thing. And I feel safe here, tucked away behind the lime green door in my nan's quirky purple house, two strange ladies who belong under the same roof.

Nan hugs me, but she also peeks over my shoulder at me. "Changing the subject, we should probably discuss my alibi."

My brow furrows. "For what?"

"Well, I'm not saying that I plan to run Elena Greene over in the Red Stripe parking lot next time I see her. But I'm not *not* saying that, either."

For the first time in days, I smile.

20. Small Town in Slow Motion

ALYSSA

Here I am, sitting on the hood of my car, underneath the water tower, all alone.

A couple of hours ago, I texted Emma and begged her to meet me. She didn't reply, but I came out here anyway. The sun is trying to shine, but hazy gray clouds blot the sky. Sometimes, spring in Indiana is daffodils and tulips, but it's also sheets of rain and impotent thunder.

I look at my phone again. No texts from Emma, and I've already waited fifteen minutes longer than the time I proposed. She doesn't owe me anything; I know that. I just—she asked me to look her in the eyes and tell her that I knew nothing about the prom switch. There's the thinnest gap of time between getting out of school and Mom getting home from work, and it's getting thinner by the minute.

A cold wind blows across the fields, and I pull my hands into my coat sleeves. In my bones, I know she's not coming, but I wait just a little longer. Just in case. The gaping hole in my heart won't close until I have a chance to see her. Talk to her. Explain. I've practiced this talk more than I practiced coming out to my mom—which is a huge part of the problem, I admit.

The wind whips my hair around my face, and strands of it stick in the tracks of my tears. She's not coming, and that's fair, I tell myself. Because it's true. That doesn't mean there's no hurt involved. I fought for her as hard as I could, and yes, I screwed up . . . but the fact that she believes I knew about the prom switch feels like a hot poker in my belly. I would never, and I thought she knew me better than that.

Just then, an engine's buzz catches my attention. I turn, looking in both directions. About a mile off, I see a little dark spot that could be a car heading this way. My throat tightens as it comes closer, closer, and I jump to my feet when I recognize the familiar shape of Nan's Beetle. They only have the one car, so Emma doesn't usually drive—but it's Emma behind the wheel now.

She pulls in next to me and slowly steps out. Bundled in a blue hoodie and a pair of blue sweats, she looks like she's surfacing for the first time in days. She even squints at the sun a little as she approaches me. Dark circles ring her eyes, and I'm guessing that beanie she's wearing is hiding bedhead. Stuffing the keys into her hoodie pocket, Emma keeps her hands in there as well.

Uneasily, I shift. Her whole body is closed off, and her face is stony. She stops more than a foot away from me. Even though I didn't expect her to throw herself into my arms, I guess I didn't think she would be so walled off. It's fair, I tell myself. No matter how much it hurts, it's fair.

"Thank you for meeting me," I say, fighting the urge to touch her. "I didn't know if you would."

Sharply, Emma shrugs. "I didn't either. What do you want?"

Wow, okay. My brain whispers, *This is fair*, but my heart protests. She's treating me like a stranger, and whether I deserve it or not, it's painful. I'm so used to her warmth that this iciness makes her into a stranger. Drawing myself up, I say, "Okay, well, first, I guess I want to say I'm sorry."

"You *guess*?"

I can't help it. I step closer. "I mean I *am*. I'm so, so sorry."

Emma bites her lip, then narrows her eyes. "What are you sorry for, exactly? Actually, just tell me: Were you in on it?"

I throw myself closer still and see the agony in her eyes. The video she made on prom night plays on an endless loop in my head. It's just hard to make it better when I can't hold her. When I can't squeeze her hands and kiss her tears away. "I swear to you, I wasn't. I didn't know about it until I got there. My mother rented a limo and threw me in it. I had no idea."

With a tip of her head, Emma considers me. There's bitterness in the curve of her lips. "Nobody told you. Not even your new BFFs?"

"What?"

"Shelby and Kaylee? You guys looked like you were having a pretty good time to me. They didn't mention anything about the big plan?"

"They are *not* my friends," I say furiously. "My mother *thinks* they are. She set everything up."

Emma looks away, weak sunlight glinting off her glasses. Her skin is so gray, except where the wind rasps pink into her cheeks. She looks like a porcelain doll, fragile and painted in stark colors. "And somehow, your mom planned a whole second prom and you had no idea."

"Emma," I say, spreading my hands. Pleading. "You know me."

When she turns back to me, I see her swallow hard. She's trying not to cry. No, she looks like she's trying not to blow away in the wind. "Do I?"

Catching her shoulders, I step close. Close enough that I smell her skin and feel her warmth. My body burns up with the sudden contact. It's been so long; it's been too long. "You do. I'm a coward, I know, I put things off too long, but you know what you mean to me!"

For the first time ever, Emma doesn't catch me up in her hands. They stay in her hoodie pocket, hidden and protected.

"No, I don't." Her voice has no edge to it; it's defeated. "I've had a lot of time to think, and I'm like . . . maybe I'm just an experiment to you. Or maybe you're trying to piss off your mom, I don't know."

Stung, I step back. "An experiment? What else, Emma? Are you wondering if this is just a *phase*?"

Emma's eyes flash. "That's not what I meant and you know it."

"It's what you said." I let go of her.

The stones fall, and suddenly Emma's expression collapses. She moves, in mourning, running her hands through the grief tangled in her hair. "Do you know what it was like standing there in that *stupid* dress alone in the gym? Knowing that people got together and planned the best way to hurt me? To humiliate me? I mean, the only thing you guys left out was a bucket of pig's blood!"

"It had to be awful," I sob, tears shaking through me.

"It was. But the worst part was that you didn't come. Even though you knew what happened, you didn't come. You didn't hold my hand, or take me out of there, you just let it happen."

It takes two tries to find my voice. "I couldn't come."

"You *should* have."

"I should have, but I couldn't. You know what my mother's like," I say, and I reach for her again.

This time, Emma flinches away from me. The wall comes back up, and she nods. "Yep. I do. I saw her on the news. She's trying to make it sound like I'm the bad guy. Like I called 1-800-Broadway and asked Barry and Dee Dee to come out here to destroy prom for everybody."

"I saw Mr. Glickman at Walmart," I say stupidly. "He was trying to change people's minds about you."

Emma seems rattled by this. But then she shakes her head and shrugs. "Whatever. Good luck with that. Look, I'm going to make another video. I'm going to tell the whole story. Will you do it with me?"

The question catches me off guard. I have a feeling the whole story is going to paint a huge target on my mother's back. And I know she's been a monster.

But I also know I listened to her this morning, leaving a message for my father again. Telling him how much she misses him and how much I need him. Admitting that things here aren't perfect and haven't been perfect since he left.

I don't know how to explain to Emma that I agree with her and I'm on her side, but I also still, despite everything, love my mother. So what I say, instead, is a weak and anemic "I want to, but . . ."

Emma smiles ruefully. "You know what, Alyssa? I believe you have feelings for me, but I can't do this anymore. It hurts too much."

Even though it doesn't come as a shock, it still hits like one. It feels like a sonic boom, shattering the sky. "Is this . . . Are you breaking up with me?"

Neither of us says anything. Emma looks into the wind, baring her face. I wrap my arms around myself tightly and wait. I will her to say no, I pray she says no.

"Yes," Emma says, punctuating it with a nod. "We're done. This is done."

And even though I want to throw myself at her and step in front of her car and beg her to stay, instead, I watch her walk away. She backs out, and as her car moves farther and farther away from me, all I want to do is scream and scream, until my voice shears into ribbons and disappears completely.

I have done nothing but achieve, jump through hoops, and put on smiles. And it's not enough. The blue ribbons and first-place trophies, my extracurriculars and my Sunday school class—I have done every single thing my mother wanted . . . for nothing. Because she's never going to stop wanting me to be perfect Alyssa Greene, and I'm never going to actually be her. Never.

Slumping against the hood of my car, I cover my face with my hands and start to cry. The one thing that was mine, the one beautiful thing that I chose, that made me feel whole and human and alive, just drove away.

And I let her.

21. Look to the Western Sky

EMMA

By the time I get home, I have no more tears left to cry. And this time, I really mean it.

This past month has been the hardest of my life, and that includes being kicked out of the house by my parents when I was fourteen, and my really unfortunate mullet phase. I'm not happy and I'm not over it, but boy, have I learned a lot.

For one, I learned that it's possible to sideline myself from my own life.

And I also learned that it's possible to convince yourself you're happy with a scrap when everybody else has the whole meal. I finally understand what they mean when people ask if the ends justify the means. Barry and Dee Dee were on my side for all the wrong reasons. Maybe Principal Hawkins was, too.

My heart is broken, but it's still beating. My town turned on me, but I survived it. I'm done waiting for my life to start. I'm over being a pawn in other people's games.

So when I pull in and see Barry and Dee Dee's rental car in front of the house, I say *bring it*. If Alyssa's to be believed, Barry thinks he's still fighting the good fight on my behalf. And you know what? Maybe he is, but I'm going to fight my own battles from here on out.

Inside, Nan sits with Barry and Dee Dee—and she jumps right up when I come in. "Emma, they have something they'd like to talk to you about. But if you're not interested in hearing it . . ."

I look from Nan to Barry, and his expression is so tentative. So hopeful. Now I remember why I trusted him so easily. I've seen that look on my own face in the mirror; I don't think he was lying when he said he knew what it was like for me and Alyssa. He probably told me a lot of truths when he swept into my life. He just didn't bother to mention that his motives weren't pure.

But Barry doesn't speak first. Dee Dee does. Of course she does. Sweeping out of the chair, she gathers the spotlight around her, even if it's just in her own mind. Pressing a hand to her chest, she says, "If I may. We have to admit that we have made matters worse. And I think the best thing we can do for Emma is to go home and put it all behind us."

Barry cuts a look in her direction. It's pretty clear there's been some discussion, and it's also pretty clear that leaving right now is not what they discussed. Imperiously, Barry tells her, "We're not leaving."

"We are *always* not leaving!" Dee Dee moans.

"We are staying until we fix this," Barry says with authority. "We're going to turn this around, Emma."

I wonder what they think there is left to turn around at this point. The prom is over. My senior year is almost done.

Most frustratingly, they've shown up and written yet another script without sharing it with me. This isn't going to happen again—I don't care about their plans. I think I know what I'm going to do next, and if they're going to be a part of it, they're going to follow. Not lead. And they're *not* going to follow until they cough up some remorse. "Okay, first of all. You two? You owe me an apology."

Dee Dee looks like I just started speaking Martian. "I did apologize."

"No," Nan says, faintly amused. "You said you made things worse."

"Which is an acknowledgment of wrongdoing," Dee Dee insists. She looks to me. "We failed to get you to prom."

"Still not an apology," Nan singsongs.

I step in, because Nan's enjoying this way too much. "And it's not what you should be sorry for anyway. You didn't come to help me. You came to help yourselves."

"Help me, help you," Dee Dee says airily. "What's wrong with that? People who need people are the luckiest people in the world, don't you know?"

Barry raises his voice, swiping his hands through the air. "Emma, I'm sorry. I'm sorry that we took your story and wrapped ourselves in it like a pashmina on an autumn day. It was wrong, we know that, and now . . . we'd like to help you. Just for you. I want to invite you and your nan to come back to New York with me. Now, or when you graduate. I have a darling little walk-up, Manhattan-adjacent—"

Dee Dee snorts. "Oh please, you live in Queens!"

Barry sends a poisonous glare at Dee Dee, then rolls his

head to look back at me, picking up where he left off. "With plenty of room. Come to stay. Come to NYU. Emma, you'll love the city. And New York City will love you back."

There are so many times I would have jumped at that offer in the past—some of them not even that long ago. It's tempting—more than tempting. It sounds like a miracle, a transformation better than a Gregg Barnes color-changing dress. It would be a whole new world, and a whole new me, and a whole new life.

But I want mine.

"That's . . . I mean, that's huge, Barry, but you know what? If every gay kid in Indiana leaves, then that means every gay kid in Indiana has to do this alone."

Nan murmurs something, I don't catch what. But her face is bright and warm, full of pride. She winks at me and gives me a little approving nod. All along, I've had her. I've never been entirely alone. And as far as I'm concerned, the next kid gets me on their side—if they want it.

"Then a press offensive," Barry says. "We'll get you on Fallon."

"How the hell are you going to get her on Fallon?" Dee Dee asks.

"I'll figure it out," Barry says through gritted teeth. He turns back to me. "You'll be the face of this story, not that PTA witch sucking up all the airtime right now. We'll get you on TV so you can show the world who this story is really about."

They're doing it again. It's almost funny; like, they can't stop taking up all the air in the room. They're literally trying right now, and failing so hard. And you know what? It makes me smile. These absolute teaspoons have been floating around being famous for so long, they don't know how to adult like normal people anymore.

"Okay, guys," I say, trying to back them down like two over-sized Siberian tigers in a Las Vegas show ring. "I wouldn't do Fallon if my life depended on it. I'm still mad that he played pet the Nazi. I'd consider Kimmel—"

"My ex-husband knows Kimmel," Dee Dee says quietly, like she just volunteered for dental surgery. "He's been dying to get the house in the Hamptons from me for years."

"Mmm, he has," Barry says agreeably.

Dee Dee's jaw is so tight, a muscle in her neck pops out when she says, "Do you know how many Broadway cruises I had to book to pay for that house? I'd rather suck my own eyes out with a vacuum cleaner than call that leech . . ."

We all watch her; this seems like a monologue, but who knows if it's the end? I think there must be something that comes next, and I'm right.

"But I will. If I have to." Dee Dee swallows the knot in her throat and reaches for my hand. "If you want me to."

Shaking my head, I squeeze her hand. "I don't want you to give up your house, Dee Dee."

She collapses with a faint *Thank god* and peeks at me through the dramatic hand across her brow. "Go on, then."

"I'm going to take a stand. And you know what? I owe you guys a thank-you for coming out here. My life was blowing up with or without you, and at least you gave it some zazz."

"That's not what that means," Dee Dee whispers, then puts on an attentive face. "I'm listening!"

My hands start to shake, and my heart feels like a Jell-O mold in the trunk of a car. It wiggles like crazy; it might even come apart. But even though it's hard to get a whole breath, I'm not going to change my mind. I won't back down.

I look at my nan, who has always had my back, and Barry, who really does know what all of this is like, and even Dee Dee, who can be forcibly nudged in the right direction. I really look at them, and everything instantly clears.

"I'm doing this my way. I'm going to record a video, and I'm putting it on my channel. I have a *lot* more subscribers now. And thanks to Mrs. Greene, people keep hitting it, looking for more of the story."

"That's true," Dee Dee says.

"And considering how much we screwed this up, you probably know better than we do," Barry agrees.

I sit on the coffee table in front of them, an offense that would normally get me told off, but *good*, by my nan. But this time, I get a raised eyebrow and curiosity about what comes next. Clasping my hands together, I nod as the plan forms in my mind.

"I'm going to do my thing. And some people in town are going to listen, and they may even cry because they'll realize what they did was wrong. And there will be shouting and meetings, and there will be a reckoning.

"It'll spread to other towns and other cities and other states. Shouting and meetings and reckonings, and maybe next year, there will be a kickass prom in Edgewater, Indiana, for everybody, no matter who they are, no matter who they love."

So far, the making-people-cry part of this plan is working. Nan is dewy, and Barry is outright sobbing. Even Dee Dee does one razor-sharp swipe beneath one eye before her mascara streaks her cheek. Normally, I'd feel bad about leaving people in tears, but I'm proud of these. I earned them. I worked for them.

Barry reaches for my hands, and I let him take them. "Emma, that would be wonderful."

"And you know what? When that happens, Barry? I want you to be my date."

"What about—"

"We broke up," I say, and a sudden well of hurt rises up through the optimism.

"Oh, honey," he says.

I nod. This time next year, we'll both be at college and I'll be a memory. Maybe one she'll keep in a shoebox and pull out from time to time—or maybe one that she'll bury deep and pretend she never had.

I don't know. And I hate that. But I can't make her do something she doesn't want to do. I can't make her be who I want her to be. Alyssa is Alyssa, and she has to find her own way.

So I shrug that aside and tell Barry, "Anyway, this will be a prom for every kid who never got theirs, and that includes you."

"Can I wear the silver tux I never wore? I still have it." Barry looks into the distance. "It needs renovations, but I happen to know—"

Nan, Dee Dee, and I all say, "Tony Award–winning costume designer Gregg Barnes!" at the same time.

"You all think you're sooo funny," Barry says, but he laughs softly. Squeezing my hands, he asks, "So when are we—when are *you* making this video? You're going to do all the work, but the least we can do is make sure you get all the attention you deserve."

Standing up, I say, "I'm going to go do it now. I've been working on a lot of music lately, and I know what I'm going to lead with."

"Godspeed," Dee Dee cries.

Barry salutes me. "And good luck."

22. For Good

ALYSSA

It's a little terrifying when I get to school and everyone is on their phone.

Technically, there are rules against having our phones out in the hallways, even though we all sneak from time to time. But this is a full-out insurrection.

As I move through the hall, people are clumped in groups, watching something together. I hear tinny sounds that might be music, but it's hard to tell with so many of them playing at once.

Turning slowly, I spin the combination to get into my locker when Shelby appears out of nowhere to glom onto me. Her face is pink and shiny with tears, but her makeup is perfect. When she throws her arms around me, she does it precisely, part drama and part genuine emotion. I think. It's hard to tell with Shelby sometimes.

"Oh. My. God," Shelby says, sniffling on my shoulder. "Did you see Emma's video?"

I feel every pore in my body close up. It would be so nice to sink into my sweater and turn into a small gray stone, but unfortunately, I'm the student council president, not the student council magician. Emma's prom video is burned into my mind. Over and over, it plays in my head, stuck there like a song. "I watched it on prom night, Shelby. Why?"

"Nooooo," she keens into my ear, squeezing me tighter. "The new one. Oh my god, I can't believe you haven't seen it. Here. Watch it. Watch!"

Shelby shoves her phone in front of me. I have to lean my head back so I can focus on the screen as she keeps pushing it closer. Finally, I take the thing from her. If I'm going to be forced to watch my ex-girlfriend's latest vlog on heartbreak, I'd prefer to do it from a reasonable distance.

Like an octopus, Shelby snakes an arm around me and pushes play. "Watch!"

"I am," I tell her, annoyed. I mean, I'd rather not, but apparently, I have no choice. And what the heck, I probably deserve it. I mentioned a while back that I am the worst person in the world, and the last two days have done nothing to change my opinion on that.

After a little ad plays, Emma's face fills the screen. The ache in my chest grows, because she looks better than the last time I saw her. Under the water tower, her skin was gray and her lips slate and her eyes bloodshot from crying. She wore every inch of her agony on her face, but she looks fine in this video. She looks *good*. And all I can think is *Oh god, she's already over me.*

The screen blurs, but I stand there anyway. Shelby breathes hotly on my neck as she re-watches, too. Her fingers dig into my shoulders, and her weight threatens to pull me off balance. Or maybe *I'm* just off balance, because Emma sits there in her lavender bed, beneath her green walls, and explains everything from the beginning.

As she speaks, her fingers touch the guitar strings without playing. They move by some memory, as she explains how the PTA threatened to cancel prom if she brought her girlfriend. How Mr. Glickman and Ms. Allen showed up to protest. How the PTA decided to hold a fake prom just for her. Her fingers strum silent chords; her shoulders move with music that's just in her head. And I realize for the first time:

She never once outed me. She never told anyone that her girlfriend went to the other prom. That her girlfriend's mother is the reason this all got started and ended up so out of hand. She never blamed me; she never named me. She never even mentioned that we agreed to go together and I backed out on her.

All this time, she's been protecting me, and I didn't even see it until now.

And then, she plays. The silent chords suddenly have voice, and she sings words that she *said* to me what seems like a million years ago.

I don't want to start a riot
I don't want to blaze a trail
I don't want to be a symbol
Or cautionary tale
I don't want to be a scapegoat
For people to oppose

What I want is simple
As far as wanting goes

To my shock, Shelby starts to sing along quietly, sniffling between lines.

I just want to dance with you
Let the whole world melt away
And dance with you
Who cares what other people say?
And when we're through
No one can convince us we were wrong
All it takes is you and me
And a song.

When Emma stops singing, I can't see her face anymore. Tears cloud my vision, and I can barely hear her voice over my own sobs. I wanted so badly to give her all of that, and I couldn't. I failed.

I'm not the perfect student, I'm not the perfect daughter, and I'm definitely not the perfect girlfriend. I'm the worst person in the world, and—

"Do you hear that, Alyssa?" Shelby asks, squeezing me tighter. "She just wanted to dance with you."

I try to say yes, but the only sound that comes out of my throat is a broken sob.

Shelby shakes me, then starts stroking my hair. "I'm really sorry we ruined that. We suck so hard."

If Emma were here, she'd say something like *That's why*

Kevin likes you, but something like that would never leave my lips. If Emma were here, I would hold her and dance with her, right here in this hallway. If Emma were here, I'd . . . I don't know. I'd make it up to her. I'd give anything to make it up to her somehow.

Still swaying with me, Shelby says, "I think it's really nice that she wants to try to have an everybody prom next year. I'd totally help with decorations for that. I could sew banners and make a big rainbow arch for pictures and maybe little baby cupids with rainbow diapers . . . I love rainbows!"

"Rainbows are great," I say numbly. Then Shelby fades to me; she's there, but separated by a strange, internal distance.

In my thoughts, I'm alone. And there's a ticking in my brain that feels like an idea. No, like a memory. Maybe both. Suddenly, so clearly, I hear Principal Hawkins reminding me, *Don't let perfect be the enemy of good.*

"I have to go to the principal's office," I say.

"You're not going to get in trouble," Shelby swears, dragging me into the present. "Everybody's on their phone; they can't put the whole school in detention."

"No," I say, laughing incredulously. "I need to talk to him. I need to . . . You said you'd help set up and decorate, right?"

Confused, Shelby nods. "Um, yeah?"

"Can you get the rest of the squad on board?" I ask her. "And the basketball teams, too?"

Shelby blinks at me. "Probably . . . ?"

"All right, do that." I peel out of her grip but grab her arms. "I have to go."

And then I plant a kiss on her cheek and run. The halls are

full of Emma's song, echoing everywhere. Probably, certainly, there are people mocking it. But I see more people crying because of it. Touching their hearts and watching again.

Butcher paper posters on the wall flap as I run by, and when I burst into the front office, the secretary yelps and jumps a little. Her face is tear-streaked, too. I can't see what's on her monitor, but I can guess.

"I need to see Principal Hawkins," I say.

"I can check and see if he's busy—" she starts, but I ignore her and head straight there. Through the window, I see he's on the phone, so I *do* knock first. But I also let myself in without waiting for an answer. Then, I lean back against the door to shut it *and* hold it closed. I'm not going to be dragged away by security or the school secretary.

Calmly, Principal Hawkins tells the person on the other line that he'll call back, and he resets the receiver. With raised brows, he leans back in his chair and steeples his hands. "Miss Greene."

"Principal Hawkins," I say breathlessly. "Have you seen Emma's new video?"

He nods once, slowly. "I have."

"You let the PTA use the gym for free, right?"

"I do."

Throwing my arms wide, I burst out, "I want to use it to throw another prom. Not just for Edgewater. For anybody who wants to come, for free."

Surprise barely registers on Principal Hawkins's face; instead, it rises, then falls to a more general kind of concern. "I think it's a lovely idea, Miss Greene, but you know we don't have the funds for something like that. The DJ, the food, the decorations . . ."

"The cheerleaders are already on board. They're going to help put everything together," I say, and I'm going to believe in my heart that it's not a lie. "The guys on the team, too. And I think I have a pretty good idea where we might be able to get some funding. I just need you to say yes."

Principal Hawkins rubs his palms together. "The PTA may still protest."

"Fine," I say. "Let them."

"Your mother's likely to take serious issue with this."

Ugh, that hits me right in the chest. It's a solid blow, but I'm not perfect. I'm going to stop trying for perfect. And that means standing up to my mother and making her understand that nothing we do is going to change Dad. He's gone; he's not coming back. It's time Mom faced that. I steel myself and say, "Almost definitely she will, sir."

Principal Hawkins considers me for a long moment. He seems a little older than he did at the start of the year. More gray in his hair, a few more lines in his face. It's possible that his older and wiser self will say no. That he's not going to continue to feed the promtroversy fire. The reporters have started to go home.

But he doesn't say that. Instead, he rolls his chair under his desk. He pats a few piles of paper, then opens a drawer. His silence is torture as he fingers through file folders one by one. Finally, he produces one and smooths it open on his desk. Taking a single sheet from it, he picks up a pen and starts to write.

"Principal Hawkins?" I say softly.

"Alyssa Greene, student council," he murmurs to himself, writing. Then he looks up at me. "And you're reserving the gym for which date?"

Clapping a hand over my mouth, I barely contain my shriek.

We. Are. Doing. This!

23. Pride in the Name of Love

EMMA

I'm going back to school today, and I'm going to be seen.

First, I'm definitely seen by the news cameras camped in the cornfield across the road. There are orange cones and striped barriers holding them back, but they surge when I get out of Nan's car. Kissing Nan on the cheek, I back out of the car and then turn as quickly as I can. I don't want to stare into all those glass eyes and lose my nerve.

Hefting my backpack onto my shoulders, I stare at the front doors for a long moment. Deciding to give up fear is one thing. Actually doing it is . . . daunting. My throat's all dry, and my chest is tight. I clutch the strap of my backpack and stiffen up my spine.

This place is just a pile of bricks—sure, full of people who thought it was clever to strangle a teddy bear in my honor, but it's just a place. A place in my hometown, where I was born, where I've grown up. I belong here.

I pull out my phone and check Emma Sings one last time before heading unto the breach. The woozy, swirling sensation in my head reaches its peak when I see the stats. More than six million views. Six. Million. Views. I'm pretty sure that's more people listening to my song than bought Kanye's last album.

More important than the numbers are the people in the comments. So many strangers with stories like mine. They reach out across the distance, saying sorry, saying me too, saying I love you. Barry was right, we do get to make our own families, and mine is growing exponentially.

My family's full of people from near and far, whose faces I've never seen but whose hearts I share. Who want to come to a prom that welcomes everybody. Who just want to dance with somebody, romantically and aromantically, and just *be*.

The biggest shock is that my new family has people from my school in it. From good old James Madison High in Edgewater, Indiana, cheering me on.

Shelby and Kevin both posted, weirdly enough (and the timestamps show them commenting within a minute of each other, so apparently this was a group activity), and so did some of the teachers. Even Principal Hawkins braved the electronic wilds to write, "I'm proud of you."

I'm walking through these doors on my own, but I'm not alone.

I stuff my phone back into my pocket, take a deep breath, and jump. Well, push. Push the doors open into the Hall of Champions.

The trophy cases gleam, and the yearbook committee has a table set up in the middle. That weird industrial-slash-teenage-hormone smell washes over me. My body wants to turn and run. It's got a little panic party going on in the limbs, urging me to *go, go, go* and never come back.

Instead, I walk forward. And as I melt into the morning crowds, the weirdest thing happens. People look at me and . . . say hi.

"Hi, Emma," Breanna says, giving me a little wave. "I love your video!"

"Thanks," I say, smiling in confusion.

Then confusion turns to wonder, because people keep on being nice. Like, guys from the basketball team say hi without snickering. Two cheerleaders wave poms at me when I pass, singing *hiIIiiIiii* like it's a ritual greeting.

Out of nowhere, the president of Key Club falls into step with me. Key Club kids are the busy little volunteers who hold pancake breakfasts to raise money for needy families and volunteer to weed medians in town, that kind of thing. Last year, they repainted old people's houses for free. I think, but I'm not sure, that they grow up to be Kiwanis Club members. Or they become Khaleesi, mothers of dragons. I'm not clear on that.

Anyway, I've seen this chick around, obviously, and I'm pretty sure her name is Dana Sklar. But we've literally never said two words to each other. Ever.

"Okay, you have to know," Dana tells me, clutching her books to her chest, "that you are amazing. The kind of outreach you're doing for LGBTQ teens online just melts my heart."

For a second or maybe two, I wait for her to turn this into a punking. Surely that was the windup, and the punch line should be along any second. Annny time now. Slowly, I realize she's not kidding. She really means it.

Incredulity turns to a little spark of happiness, and I say, "Thanks, that means a lot."

"And if you want," she goes on, pulling out her phone, "I have a bunch of stuff on fundraising and how to put together an event and stuff like that. I can email it to you, if you want?"

"That would be great," I say, my face growing hot. Somehow, this conversation is a really real thing that I'm not hallucinating. It's hard to get my head around it, but I have to admit that my video did this. *I* did this. "Thank you, really. Just, you can send it to enolan dot sings at gmail dot com."

With quite possibly the swiftest thumb in the county, Dana puts my address into her phone and then nods at me. "Okay, great! I'll get that to you. And if you ever want to come to a meeting or anything . . ."

Probably, I do not, but who knows? Maybe I do? After a few more pleasantries, Dana melts back into the general haze of people hanging out in the halls before classes start. I look down and realize my hands are shaking. I don't know what that is—maybe adrenaline? Maybe terror? Maybe . . . excitement? All I know is that my stomach is full of weasels, and they're chasing their tails at top speed.

When I turn down the hall where my locker is, I see something stuck to it. The weasels get drunk and start trashing the place as I approach.

Look, it can't possibly be any worse than the bear, and the lotion, and the salad dressing. This is my school, too; I belong. I'm not going to use my locker, because I'm not *stupid*—but I'm going to walk past it. I'm going to look.

And when I do, I stop short and almost cry. Right there, in

the hall, surrounded by people who slow down to look my way.

Someone has pasted a glittery rainbow, complete with clouds and a sun peeking out, at the top of my locker. And underneath it, there's a long piece of butcher paper cut to look like a scroll. They even drew in the loops at the top and bottom.

On it, in calligraphy, someone wrote out the words to my song. Someone in this school sat and listened to my video long enough to get all the lyrics down. And then they scripted them in beautiful swirls on this faux parchment. Then they drew musical notes around them and dusted the whole thing with more glitter.

I cover my mouth with my hand, because I feel tears threatening. People are looking at me, so I manage to hold it in. But when I glance at them, they're *smiling*. They're here, in this moment, sharing it with me.

Subtly, I bite the tip of my thumb. Really hard. So hard that I'm like, *What the hell, Emma?* But I'm rewarded with a jolt of pain which means *Yup, I'm awake.* This is actually happening. Because I have no idea who did this, I mumble thanks at the people around me. Just anybody in thanking distance, you know?

Deep inside, I almost wish that somebody would walk by and call me a name. Because that? That would be normal. I expect that, not kindness. Not acceptance. It's genuinely frightening to stand here and accept that maybe my song (and, okay, a tiny bit of Barry and Dee Dee's shenanigans) might have really changed them. There's no way it reached everybody; realistically, I know that. But, oh my god, it changed *some*.

This moment feels so fragile, and I feel so clumsy. But I

hold it close to my heart. Carefully and gently. Opening up is the hardest thing I've ever done, but slowly, I lift my head and stand there, feeling more myself than I ever have. When I look around, I meet everyone's eyes. I am Emma Nolan, Hoosier, lesbian, and human being.

And I am proud.

24. Begin Again

ALYSSA

I hear their voices before I see them. I think people probably say that a lot about Mr. Glickman and Ms. Allen. Loud or not, I'm glad they accepted my invitation.

"I can't believe we're back in this place," Ms. Allen says. "In my memoirs, I'm calling this chapter 'Groundhog Day.'"

Mr. Glickman replies immediately. "I thought that was the title of the chapter about your husbands?"

Between their sniping, I hear a low voice of reason. That has to be Principal Hawkins, and I'm glad that he's here. Not that he wouldn't be, but Mr. Glickman and Ms. Allen make me nervous, and I'm kind of glad I've never been alone with them. Their hearts are in the right place; it's all the flying jazz hands that scare me.

When they come into the gym, I wave from my carefully arranged table. There's a laptop, a projector, a stack of handouts, and a diorama. The diorama was probably unnecessary, but I haven't made one since seventh grade (*Scene at Gallows Hill in Salem, 1692*), and I'm kind of good at them.

"Hi, thank you for coming, hi!"

Next to me, the school's ancient laptop starts humming. It had better not blow up before I finish my presentation; quickly, I say a silent prayer for technology. Then I smile as brightly as I can as the adults approach. Ms. Allen's heels click on the hardwood floor in a way that I'm sure would send Coach Strickland into fits.

She's wearing what seems to be one of a thousand pantsuits she owns, and I'm starting to really respect her dedication to a look. This one has no sequins, but the red fabric is shot through with silver thread. The bottoms of her shoes are blood-red, too, and I marvel. Those are probably the only pair of Louboutins ever to grace Edgewater, Indiana.

Mr. Glickman is casual in a jacket and tie, and when he gets closer, I squint at the pattern on the tie. Little white outlines of hair—no, I get it. Wigs. Wigs of all shapes and sizes, arrayed in a graceful grid pattern.

They're so out of place, it's funny, and yet . . . it almost seems like this won't be home anymore if they leave. I offer my hand when they approach. "Hi, I'm Alyssa Greene, the student council president. Thank you for coming. Thank you, thank you for coming, thank you, Principal Hawkins."

As soon as I say my name, Mr. Glickman goes frosty. He looks at me down his nose and crosses his arms over his chest. Well, I guess somebody in the room knows that I'm the ex-girlfriend. That's okay, pretty sure everyone is going to know in a couple of minutes.

I pass out copies of the agenda, and their eyes skim the page. Lots of white space, for easy skimming. Ms. Allen squawks about halfway down, but Principal Hawkins puts a (very familiar!) hand on her shoulder and says, "Please, hear her out."

Picking up the clicker, I advance my PowerPoint to the first slide. It's a still from Emma's video, where she sings and shares her vision for a prom for everyone one day. "As of this morning, more than six million people have viewed Emma's video about an inclusive, open prom."

Mr. Glickman sniffs. "That video just kills me. It's better than the one about the guy being reunited with the lion he raised from a cub."

"Don't bring that up," Ms. Allen says, also sniffling. "I can't even think about it."

Exploding with emotion, Mr. Glickman waves at the screen with Emma's face on it. His eyes glimmer with tears, and he fans his face. "She said she had a plan, and look at her. She's so smart, that kid."

I know if I don't cut him off, it'll be ages before I can finish my pitch. And I don't have ages. Shelby and Kevin just showed up at the gym doors, and they're slinking in to sit on the bleachers. Some of the Golden Weevils basketball team slide in, along with their cheerleader cohort, more of them than I expected, actually. (Notably absent? Kaylee and Nick.) Everyone else settles in, whispering.

I can't make out what they're saying, but it's not important. I raise my voice, and fortunately, it carries in a mostly empty gym. "She asked for one thing, and I think we can make it happen. Not next year, this year."

Power-clicking through my presentation, I go on, trying

not to focus on Mr. Glickman's and Ms. Allen's faces. If I pay too much attention to their reactions, I won't be able to get this all out.

"As you know, the school has no budget for dances, and traditionally, funding has come from outside sources. Now, I have secured the school gym as the event site for free. I've even created a diorama to show the potential design of the dance. And I have a team of students prepared to help decorate. Shelby? Kevin?"

They stand up and cheer and hoot from the bleachers.

"What we're missing, Ms. Allen, Mr. Glickman, is money. Now, I could host a GoFundMe and, with as many views as Emma's getting on her video, probably get that money in time for a prom next fall. I'm not interested in next fall. I'm interested in this year, this place, two weeks from now."

Mr. Glickman shifts from ice to fire. He all but vibrates with excitement. "It's Mickey and Judy time. We'll build this prom with blood and hair if we have to."

"Wait," Ms. Allen says. "According to this cute little line item, you're looking for *fifteen thousand dollars?*"

Even though I feel weak hearing the number aloud, I nod my head. "I've priced everything out. That's a good DJ from Evansville, catering instead of homemade treats, decorations, a photographer, and souvenirs."

Mr. Glickman holds up a hand. "How much are we talking if we really do this up? No hay bales and a cutout cow. A real A-level, Tony Award–worthy prom?"

This time, when I break into a smile, it's genuine. I was hoping someone would ask. I hand them the second printout.

"For everything I already mentioned, plus lighting, special effects, flowers, and professional decorations, thirty thousand dollars."

Ms. Allen swoons. "Jesus."

Without hesitating, Barry reaches into his front pocket and produces a wallet. He hands me a credit card, black, with obvious signs of wear around the edges.

"There's fifteen thousand dollars on there," he says. "That's my limit. It's a long story, but I had to declare bankruptcy after my self-produced gritty reboot of *Peter Pan*."

Principal Hawkins blinks. "That's a lot of money. You're sure?"

"Listen," Barry says, raising his voice so the kids in the bleachers can hear as well. Not that they're paying attention, but if they were, they'd be able to hear him. "We failed at the abstract singing and speechifying. This is concrete. This is buying. This is the American way."

Nodding slowly, Principal Hawkins produces his wallet. "It's not much, but I can put down two thousand."

"Thank you," I say, starting to get misty. This is going to happen. We already have enough for the hometown version of the prom, so it's on, regardless. At that moment, all three of us—Mr. Glickman, Principal Hawkins, and I—look to Ms. Allen expectantly.

Stiffening, Ms. Allen returns the looks. "What?" she says finally.

"Dee Dee, come on." Barry cozies up to her. "I know you have an AmEx with no limit."

Principal Hawkins gazes into Dee Dee's eyes. "I know you

have it in you. All our talks at Applebee's? I know you want to do the right thing."

There have been talks at Applebee's? Talks, plural? Apparently so, and when I look to Ms. Allen, I'm amazed.

Her face, always so studied and perfect, suddenly softens. I'd never, ever tell her this, because I think it might break her heart, but for just a second, I get a glimpse of Ms. Allen the human being instead of Ms. Allen the star. Not that they're not the same person—it's just that one aspect gets all the spotlight, and the other? Not so much.

The star reappears, and she reaches into her purse. She snaps a credit card out of the clutch like it was in a holster and hands it over. "God, why does being good cost *so much money?* Go on. Take it."

Right now, I feel like I could fly through the roof. It's like fireworks and champagne bubbles. I feel like a comet streaking across the sky. There's applause and cheering, but I am so effervescent, I barely hear it. What I *do* hear is my mother's voice cutting through it all.

"Alyssa Greene, what is the meaning of this?"

Quickly, I advance the slide on my presentation. I padded the slideshow with some extra facts on the off chance they were reluctant to donate (cough—Ms. Allen—cough). At first, my voice catches in my throat. It's terrifying, the look on my mother's face. She sees the projection screen, the slide with a big pink PROM FOR EVERYONE on it. She sees the date, the time, and all the different pride flags underneath. And she sees me, standing beneath it, just like I planned. My mother can't resist a PTA obligation, and I told her that's exactly what this was to get her here.

"Mrs. Greene," Principal Hawkins says, but I cut him off.

"I've got this," I say, with more confidence than I feel. Taking a few steps toward her, I let go of my guilt—because I'm not a perfect daughter. I let go of my fear—because I can't change who I am, and she's going to find out sooner or later. And I let go of my responsibility—I'm the *kid* here. She's the parent. It's not my job to take care of her; she's supposed to take care of me.

"I certainly hope there's an explanation," Mom says, waving a hand furiously at the screen.

Just past my mother, there's a shadow in the doorway. I know that shape. I'd know it anywhere, and I'm so glad the note pulled her out of class at just the right time, because she deserves to see this. Standing up straight, I approach my mother and offer her my hand. She doesn't take it, and it hurts, but I don't let that stop me.

"Mom, I love you. And I'm so grateful to you, for all you do for me. For all you've done for me since Dad left."

"Alyssa!" she whispers, scandalized.

I've spoken it aloud, the truth we don't discuss. But I go on. "And I know this is going to be another thing that's hard on you. But, Mom, I'm gay. I've always been gay. And to answer the questions I know you want to ask, nobody did this to me. Nobody hurt me. You didn't do anything wrong. This is who I am; I'm proud of who I am. You know everything about me, and it's been so hard keeping this from you. Too hard. I can't do it anymore. Mom, I'm gay."

Mom laughs, a sound that's wound tight with anxiety. Her eyes dart around, taking in how many people are seeing this, how many are witnessing her humiliation. I see her fighting to keep it together. To look perfect, be perfect. She fights for a smile and whispers at me again. "Alyssa, that's quite enough."

Shaking my head, I say, "No. I've put this off for way too long. And I've hurt someone so precious to me, in a way I can't ever expect her to forgive. I was Emma Nolan's date to the prom, Mom. We were supposed to go together, and I let her down."

Now my mother starts to cry. "Stop it. Just stop it. Alyssa, I'm sorry, but this is not who you really are. Whatever you're feeling, it's not real. You're young and you're confused."

"I'm not confused. I'm in love."

Mom stamps at the ground, jabbing an accusing finger at Mr. Glickman and Ms. Allen. "This is *their* fault. They're putting ideas into your head, and they're forcing me to be someone I don't want to be. You are young, you are impressionable, and I'm sick of this. This ends now."

For the first time since my mother appeared, Mr. Glickman speaks. "If you don't let her be who she is, you're going to lose her."

"Excuse me?" my mother says, all acid.

He steps closer and speaks, low and heartbroken. "I mean, she'll go away to college, and she'll forget to write. She'll move to another state and send you cards on Mother's Day. She'll come home for Christmas for a while, until she has to choose between the family she makes for herself and the family who won't accept that. And soon, you'll count the months between phone calls. The years between visits. Until one day, you'll wonder how it is that your baby left and never came home."

"I don't think—" my mother says tartly, but Mr. Glickman takes her hand.

"Trust me, Mrs. Greene. I *know*."

The gym falls silent, except for some sniffling from the bleachers. I glance over, and Shelby has buried her face against Kevin's chest. The cheerleaders clutch each other, and—well, the basketball players shuffle uncomfortably. There can only be so many miracles in one day.

My mother looks at Mr. Glickman, then she turns to me. And there it is: the face I feared, the one where I can see every hurt and every wound she's suffered in the last few years. The silver in her hair that tragedy put there, the lines on her face that I've caused. But instead of raising her voice, my mother pulls herself together and swipes her face dry.

"This is not what I hoped for you," she says. "This is going to make your life so much harder, in so many ways. And that's the last thing I ever wanted. The reason I've been trying so hard to get your father to come back is so you can have the life you *deserve*. The world isn't a forgiving place, Alyssa."

I tremble. "I know. But it doesn't change who I am."

My mother clasps my face in her hands. They're cool against my skin, but her eyes are warm. She searches my face, and she sighs.

Every muscle in my body is stretched tight, ready to snap. Is this when she gives me up? Is this when I lose my mother for good? I stand so still, it hurts, trying desperately to read the thoughts behind her eyes.

It takes her a moment to find her voice. And even then, she

stares at the floor—trying, I think, to find the words. Finally, she slowly pronounces, "Alyssa, you're my baby girl. My own gift from God. My most precious treasure."

I try to hold still, but inside, I'm squirming. I still can't tell if this is a goodbye or a hello. "Mom . . ."

She raises my face to hers. Her perfectly manicured nails brush against my temples, and she traces her thumbs against my cheeks. Then, finally, she leans in and she kisses my forehead.

Her perfume washes over me, and a million memories flood through me: making cookies with her at Christmas; snuggling beneath a blanket and watching the first snowfall of the year; waking her up in the middle of the night because I had a nightmare and being wrapped so tight, so safely in her arms that all the fear just burned away.

Right now, this moment, my fear burns away when she says, "I love you."

Clinging to her, I whisper, "I love you, too."

She hugs me, an impossibly short hug, and she steps away. Holding my gaze, she slips back and says sincerely, "We'll talk tonight."

Then she turns and walks away. She holds her head high, and her heels click efficiently across the gym floor. Her posture is impeccable, and she sweeps one stray hair back into place with a graceful hand. There's no wavering; she doesn't look back. She knows she doesn't have to. She said what she said. She loves me, and we'll talk tonight.

It hits me in a sudden wave. In a crashing of thunder. I wobble on unsteady legs, gathering my senses and my balance at the same time.

My mom knows.

The secret is out. No more lying, no more pretending. From here on out, when she looks at me, she'll see who I really am. She doesn't have the words yet, but she *knows*.

And—somehow, improbably—she still loves me.

25. Juliet in Converse

EMMA

Mrs. Greene walks past me in a cloud of brimstone and designer imposter Chanel N°5.

The last time I saw a back that straight, I was sitting in the doctor's office, staring at the tiny anatomical model she keeps on the shelf. Mrs. Greene is really rocking the vertical thoracic spine right now. Suffice it to say, I don't think I'm invited to the Greene family Thanksgiving.

And all of that joking is a strong, heavy shield for the soft, vulnerable feelings I contain. The note from the office to send me to the gym was weird, but I got here in time to hear Alyssa come out to her mother in front of a screen glowing with the words PROM FOR EVERYONE.

Barry and Dee Dee stand there with Principal Hawkins, and for some reason, most of the Golden Weevils are hanging out on the bleachers. This feels like a dream I once had, except I'm not naked, and the gym isn't also the China Garden right off I-69.

Wary, I walk inside. My boots sound so heavy, echoing low thunder as I approach Alyssa. Any minute, I expect laughter or jeers from the stands, but it doesn't come. Instead, Alyssa walks toward me, her hands clasped together almost in prayer.

I know we broke up, but that doesn't mean my unruly heart stopped loving her. How could it?

This is the girl who flirted with me at a church picnic. The girl who texted me pictures of otters in the middle of the night and whispered love in my ear. This is the girl who was brave enough to kiss me first, when I was still desperately trying to figure out if she liked me or if she *liked* me.

There's so much history written on our skin, so many firsts that will always belong to us alone. They were secret, and they were ours, and that doesn't melt away in an instant. How could it? Something so real and monumental can only be abandoned. It doesn't cease to exist.

And that's why my heart leaps up, full of strange optimism and hope, but I keep my shield close. Loving her so completely means that she can wound me with a single word. I have to protect myself, because her delicate hands still hold so much power.

As proof, Alyssa stops a few feet in front of me, and her expression steals past my shield with ease. As soon as she's close, I want to surrender. I want to throw myself into her arms and hold her again. The urge is so strong, I swear I feel her already—the warmth of her body and the silk of her skin.

You can't, I tell myself. *Just don't.*

Her dark eyes shine in the low light, and her tentative smile glows. I see her swallow nervously, her fingers squeezing together even tighter.

"What is all of this?" I ask. According to Nan, she who talks first loses, but it doesn't feel like anyone's losing today. I know Alyssa knows what I mean, but I nod toward the screen, and the team, and the . . . diorama? Anyway.

Stroking a long swirl of her dark hair behind her ear, Alyssa says, "It's for you."

"I don't get it," I say, even though I kind of do. I want to hear her say it.

"You asked for a prom where everyone was welcome, and it's going to happen. We have funding, thanks to Principal Hawkins, Ms. Allen, and Mr. Glickman; and we have a committee ready to build it, thanks to Shelby and Kevin. There's a date, and a time, and I hope you'll help us get the word out."

It's too much. Like, my brain is so full right now, it pounds against my skull. My closeted ex-girlfriend and a couple of misguided Broadway stars are bringing this to life? It was a small idea, one that I hoped would develop over time. Something that might eventually come together, something to look forward to.

I didn't think it would happen this quickly or that it would happen this way. And honestly, that's all a way of saying that I didn't think this would happen for *me*.

My lips, the lips that have kissed Alyssa's a thousand times, are numb. They barely move when I speak. "And your mother?"

Alyssa nods. "It was time. I did it for me, but I wanted you to see. I thought you deserved that much."

It's getting harder to stand so far from her. My feet take a step closer without my permission. "Are you okay?"

Alyssa hesitates, like she's taking some mental inventory

before she answers. But then she smiles softly and nods. "Yeah, I am. I have a feeling I'm going to be explaining all the other letters in the rainbow a few thousand times over the next couple of weeks, but yeah. I'm . . . I'm really okay."

I feel like I'm whispering when I say, "I'm happy for you."

Suddenly, Alyssa sweeps forward and catches my hands. She curls her arms around mine and pulls me in close. Pressed against her, I swear I feel her heartbeat on my skin again, and it makes me sweat. She's just a little bit shorter than I am, so when she leans in, her nose rests against mine, and her eyes look up into me. All the way through me.

"I love you," she says, her voice rough with emotion. "And I'm so sorry about before. None of this would have happened if I had just spoken up sooner."

Her apology makes something bloom inside me. Heat washes from my heart to all my ends and beginnings. I've wanted to hear and believe an apology since prom night, but she's taking responsibility for too much. It's just like her. Full of forgiveness, I'm also full of reason. Squeezing her hands, I shake my head. "I won't let you take the blame for things you didn't do, Alyssa. Just say, *I'm sorry I stood you up.*"

"I'm sorry I stood you up," she whispers, her breath warm on my lips.

I take that and tuck it away, deep in my heart. And then it's easy to say the words she deserves to hear, too. "I'm sorry I didn't believe you—and I'm sorry I pushed so hard. Everybody should get to come out in their own time and their own way."

Across the gym, Barry cries out, "And we're sorry, too!"

Alyssa and I laugh, turning to look at him. "For what?"

"For using you," Barry says, and Dee Dee nods. "We got blasted in the *New York Times*. They said we were narcissists, in big, bold font. And it hurt, I guess, because they were right."

This is so bizarre. Seriously, I'm back to wondering if I'm dreaming. But if I am, it's a hell of a dream. "Aren't all actors narcissists?"

Throwing her head back, Dee Dee pronounces, "Yes, but we're *really* good at it."

"We decided to look for a cause, to give us credibility. Get a little good press. We thought about building houses with Habitat for Humanity—"

Dee Dee interrupts, "But we don't actually know how to build anything."

"So maybe we're not the best human beings in the world. But we got here and got to know you and your town . . . and suddenly, that bad review didn't matter so much anymore. The truth is, yes, we came because of a bad review."

Then warmly, more warmly than I've heard Dee Dee say anything, while (alert! alert! alert!) slipping her hand into Principal Hawkins's (!!!!!!), she says, "But we stayed because of you."

From the bleachers, Shelby jumps up. "And we're sorry, too. Aren't we, Kevin?" Despite her tiny frame, Shelby hauls him up like a naughty puppy. He nods emphatically, and he gets rewarded with a very booby hug. Twined on him like ivy, Shelby says, "You deserve to go to prom, just like everybody else!"

"I thought you hated me," I say, somehow slowly tangling

around Alyssa as well. "I thought you all hated me."

"Oh, we did; Kaylee still does," Shelby says agreeably. Then she looks to Barry. "But Mr. Pecker crashed our hang at Walmart and said some stuff that made us think. He's a really good teacher."

Barry takes a tiny bow but also waves Shelby off, as if to say, *No, no, please, that's too much, you're too kind.* It cracks me up that he can take the credit and also pretend to be humble at the same time. It's like his superpower or something.

I don't know what to do with this moment. Historically, my life hasn't worked out this neatly before. It's hard to believe so many people have turned around because of a song and, apparently, a star turn in the Walmart parking lot—I'm going to have to ask about that later for sure.

Instead of blustering, or joking, or any of that, I'm just honest. Turning in Alyssa's arms, I tell her, "I don't know what to say."

"Well," she says, shyly, a little coyly, "there's this prom coming up . . ."

Fireflies light up inside me. "Uh-huh."

A question doesn't come; she doesn't even finish that sentence. Instead, Alyssa, with her reedy voice and uncertain smile, sings to me, "*I just want to dance with you, let the whole world melt away and dance with you . . .*"

And then, all around me, suddenly there are voices singing my song. Shelby sways with Kevin, and literally no one from the bleachers is in tune, but they know the words. I hear Barry and Dee Dee lift their voices, trying to out-emote each other.

Probably, Principal Hawkins sings, too, but once Dee Dee and Barry get going, it's impossible to tell.

They sing my song. They sing my words and my heart. With every note, it feels like I'm being taken apart and scrubbed new and put back together again. There's pride in there, yes, that I created something that suddenly has life outside of me.

But mostly, it's a becoming. I feel new, for the first time in years. I feel special—I feel seen and loved. Being out in Edgewater, Indiana, is something it never was before: beautiful.

My head spins, and all I can do is stare incredulously at everyone else, and melt away in Alyssa's eyes when I look to her. Here I am, back in her arms. Back where I belong, because we fit together without a single space between. My hurt and resentment and frustration burn away like phoenixes. Now they're joy and excitement and anticipation.

Alyssa frees her hands so she can lay them against my face. Her thumbs skim the curve of my lower lip; her nails rasp delicately against my cheeks. Her heat sinks into me, and I am hopelessly trapped in her gaze. Her body lifts and tightens against mine with each breath. My melody vibrates through her, and I feel the crest to each note in her arms. This is the most epic promposal in the world. Bar none, no arguing, the record is set forever.

When their voices trail off, I exhale Alyssa's name in wonder. I never wanted to let her go; I just felt like I had to. Now it feels like I should never set her free again. My cheeks flush hot, and I'm afraid my palms are sweaty, but I cling to her all the same.

Abruptly, Shelby and the cheerleaders chant, like this is

some fan fiction come to life, "Kiss, kiss, kiss, kiss!"

"A kiss is yes," Alyssa warns me.

Warning taken. That's why I engulf her in my arms and lift her off the ground, just an inch, and kiss her until we see nothing but the two of us, the edge of forever, and the end of the world.

26. Let's Put on a Show

ALYSSA

We're really lucky Mr. Glickman and Ms. Allen donated so much to the cause.

As soon as Emma posted about the new prom on her channel, we were flooded with requests for tickets. There are kids coming from all over Indiana for this dance, and a bunch who are coming from out of state. Illinois, Ohio, Kentucky—they're all coming here, so we had to get creative.

Prom won't just be in the gym; it will also extend out into the school parking lot. We cordoned off the entire thing and rented huge white marquee tents with plastic windows in them. Standing at one end of the tent, I wave both hands slowly as the basketball team unrolls four of the biggest carpets I've ever seen. They grunt and huff as they shove the rolls toward me.

"Okay," I say when they finish stomping down the curled ends to flatten them. "Next thing we need are cocktail tables. If you look at the chart I made, just follow that, and they'll be exactly where they're supposed to be. Thank you!"

I take a quick jog up to the open gym doors to peek inside.

Somehow, Shelby got all of the cheerleaders to help, including the junior team from the middle school. The Key Club is here, and National Honor Society. Most of the choir showed up, and I'm pleased that the rest of the student council turned out as well.

We need the extra hands, especially because Mr. Glickman quote, unquote called in some favors, and two days later, several huge crates arrived at the school. Better than crepe paper and plastic bunting, the crates spilled forth with huge, beautiful sheets of blue, glimmering cloth that we draped around the gym and the stage. There were two cardboard boxes in there full of foiled butterflies that flap their wings when you hang them from their invisible nylon cords.

To go along with those, there are burnished gilt lanterns for the tables and thick ropes of flickering fairy lights to string between standup lampposts that really light up.

Finally, there are massive frames with picturesque cityscapes painted on them. They're erected on casters, so they roll with ease, and on the backs are frames for lights, so the little windows will actually glow on prom night.

"*How to Succeed* hasn't run on Broadway for years," Mr. Glickman explained broadly. "They won't miss them!"

And speaking of Mr. Glickman, he's holding court at one end of the gym. Perched in a folding chair, he talks about his many, many successes on Broadway as he inflates a balloon with helium. Once it's full, he hands it off to a handful of FCK kids to tie off.

Then they go into a massive box where they shimmer in pearly, pastel rainbows. We're going to dump them into a net and hang them from the ceiling, so when we play the last song of the night, we'll pull the rope and they'll come floating down onto the dance floor. As far as finales go, it's a little bit tame, but Principal Hawkins nixed the confetti cannons.

Ms. Allen has an eye for arrangement and flow. Every so often, she claps sharply or taps one of her heels against the floor to get someone's attention. Then she walks them through the spaces between the tables. With assertive hands, she points out what needs to happen. Her assistants, mostly guys from the basketball team, follow her and shift tables and chairs until there's a perfect balance. There's no way she was ever going to pick up a table herself.

Posted at the door, Principal Hawkins supervises and signs off on deliveries. So far, he's accepted two cases of souvenir dance cards, a pallet full of pride-flag key chains in multiple orientations, several thousand pronoun pins, and now he's running down the catering receipt.

Kids are coming from so far away, we wanted to make sure they got a meal. The people from the caterers are setting up huge trays that will hold all the stuff for our taco-bowl bar. We have three huge sheet cakes, iced tea, ice water, and, yes, sherbert punch and cookies. I can't abandon tradition.

As everything comes together, I stand in the middle of the gym with my clipboard and slowly take it in. Everything looks so perfect; it's like a dream made real. One of the women from the party-lights place sets up a ladder near me. I watch as she climbs up and hefts a massive gold disco ball above her head.

Once it's secure, her assistant turns on the lights. Fractures of gold dance across the floor and along the walls. With the flickering, shifting brightness, the butterflies seem to come alive. From the far end of the gym, the DJ sends a mechanical hum through the place, then blasts us with some Ariana Grande.

The explosion of music didn't startle me, but hands suddenly around my waist from behind do. Relieved, I sink back against Emma to anchor myself and look over my shoulder. "You're not supposed to be here," I tease. "It's bad luck to see the prom before prom night."

She presses a kiss to my neck and hugs me close. "I promise, I'm not looking. But I don't need to see it to know that everything looks fantastic."

I laugh. "It's really coming together. How are the electronic tickets going?"

Emma set up an evite for up to eight hundred people, and the last I'd heard, tickets were about 60 percent claimed. It was the fairest way we could think of to invite everybody but also be realistic about the fact that we don't have unlimited space.

"All gone," she says. "And I checked with the Comfort Inn; they're pretty much booked up, too. People are actually coming, Alyssa. This is actually happening."

Before I can reply, my mother walks in. She's the last person I expected to see. Just like she promised, we talked the night I came out. It wasn't all good; she still doesn't understand why I can't just date boys. Why I can't just shove it down and be normal. She hasn't been to church in weeks because she doesn't know what to say about me.

But she also told me that she was proud of me, no matter

what. Proud of the woman I was becoming. Proud that I stand up for my principles. (Not thrilled that I stood up for them against *her*, mind you, but baby steps.)

We also talked a lot about Dad. She finally admitted he wasn't coming home. She cried, and I cried, and then I told her about Tinder. She was horrified; I probably should have started with Christian Mingle.

Emma lets her arms slip away; I appreciate that she's going easy on my mom. For all her sarcasm and sharpness, Emma's one of the most generous people I know. And one of the most forgiving, too. I doubt Mom and Emma will ever be friends, but I'm so glad she'll never make me choose between them.

Mom offers a stiff hello to Emma (which is more than I expected, actually), then looks around. Golden flecks of light dance across her face. "You're putting on quite a production here."

"We've had a *ton* of help," I say. "What's up with you? I didn't expect to see you here."

She shrugs slightly and raises the box. "I always lend the prom my grandmother's punch bowls."

Oh wow. I know how difficult this is for her, but I can see how hard she's trying. Emma steps in and offers to take the box from her. Then she slips quietly away to leave me with my mother.

This is still new, and still hard, so I make it as simple for Mom as I can. I throw my arms around her in a hug and squeeze her tight. "Thank you, Mommy."

"It's the least I could do," she says, and hugs me back.

27. Prom Night Again

EMMA

"No, sweetheart, it's walk, walk, pivot, turn!"

Once again, my house is full of Nan and Broadway. Dee Dee sits on the arm of the couch, "sampling" Nan's pound cake again, and Barry waves his hands, trying to direct me as I show off my suit.

They're already dressed in full regalia. In gold, to match the theme of the night, Dee Dee's decked out in a lamé pantsuit cut down to whoa. And Barry? He's totally wearing the silver tux he bought for the first prom he never got to attend. With teal bow tie and cummerbund, he's resisting the pound cake by ordering me around.

I duck back down the hallway to attempt this perfect runway walk he seems to think I can accomplish. And actually, I probably can. Most days, I don't think about my clothes much. They're just there to cover my body and keep me from public indecency charges.

But this outfit is different. Tonight, I feel *good*.

No gowns. Not this time. Instead, I have a black velvet

jacket that makes me feel so boss, I want to go out and sing karaoke in front of strangers. I mean, it's that epic of a jacket. I keep running my hands over my own arms, luxuriating in the warm, soft kiss of the fabric. If Alyssa and I break up again, I might date this thing. I mean, for real.

My shirt is white and fitted, with dark blue edging on the collar and sleeves. My tie is silk, patterned in dark blues and purples, a little galaxy swirling along its length. The pants are lighter blue, cut above my ankles, and made of some kind of slick material that whispers when I walk.

Barry insisted on getting everything fitted, and I have to say, he was right. Darts and tucks do make everything 150 percent more fabulous.

"Let's go," barks Barry, clapping his hands impatiently. "Let's see that walk!"

With a laugh, I throw my shoulders back for some zazz, and then I march the length of the hallway and into the living room. I walk, walk, walk, pivot, and then start laughing before I can manage the turn. It's just too much for this girl to manage.

Tumbling into the couch between Dee Dee and Barry, I look up at them both. These two. They have been the worst, best thing that ever happened to me. I still can't believe they rolled into town with picket signs and crashed a school meeting with the entire touring cast of *Godspell*.

They made things so much harder, but I can't help but look at where I am right now: dressed to the nines and waiting for my girlfriend to show up so we can go to prom together, a dance that's so much bigger than just one graduating class. None of this would have happened without them either.

I have my nan, who loves me more than anything in this world, and now I have two (occasionally misguided, definitely narcissistic) fairy godparents, and that's so much more than so many other kids get. Gratitude fills me with this sweet, golden wave, and I look to Barry, and then Dee Dee, and say, "Thank you."

"For what?" Barry says, playing it off. I know he wants to hear it.

With an arched brow, Dee Dee says, "Buying an entire prom, for one."

He gives her a look, and I laugh between them. Laying my head against Barry's shoulder, I say, "For coming to Edgewater and wrecking my life. I really needed it."

"Well," Barry says, patting my arm, "I like to think of it as renovating."

"Whatever it is, I'm glad it happened. Because I'm here, and you're here, and, oh my god, hundreds of queer kids from all over the Midwest are here . . ."

Barry smiles, but he nudges me. "Hey. Take some credit."

"Yes, take it. Most people aren't going to give it to you, so you'll have to snatch it for yourself, like nature, red in tooth and claw—" Dee Dee interrupts herself with a significant look and then credits herself, "*Tennyson: The Musical*, original Broadway cast, 19—Never mind."

Nan leans forward, her round face comforting and familiar. She's got a lavender streak in her hair for tonight, and a rainbow manicure. The whole look is pulled together with a black T-shirt that says PROM FOR EVERYONE on the front and CHAPERONE on the back. They really did think of everything.

"Dee Dee's right. You helped grow something beautiful out of something terrible, and I couldn't be prouder of you."

Rolling out of the couch to hug Nan, I hear Dee Dee tell Barry, "Did you hear that? *Dee Dee's right.*"

With a good, solid hug, Nan kisses both of my cheeks. Then she straightens my jacket, tugging the lapels and smoothing my tie. There are tears in her eyes, and I wonder if she's thinking about my dad right now. When she kept me, she lost him. I used to feel guilty about that, like I'd wrecked our family. But I don't anymore.

We all make choices, and all those choices matter. I've always been exactly who I am; he's the one who failed as a father. But that's another terrible thing that led to beautiful things for me, because I wouldn't give up my nan for anyone.

She was my champion long before Barry and Dee Dee showed up, and she's my favorite person in the world (even if she does cheat at *Super Smash Bros. Brawl*). I hope she feels the same way—I'm pretty sure she does.

My phone chirps, and it's like a siren. Everyone in the room sits up and looks toward the sound. I don't dive for it, because come on, but I do move expeditiously across the room to pluck it up. Swiping the lockscreen away, I smile at Alyssa's name, all lit up. `Turning down your street right now. Can't wait to see you!`

"Is she coming?" Dee Dee asks.

"Of course she's coming," Barry says, then looks to me nervously. "But she is coming, isn't she?"

I hold out the phone so they can see it with their own eyes. I don't blame them for asking. I barely slept last night myself.

Part of it was knowing that this huge thing is happening and all eyes are on Edgewater again (still?).

In the last two days, a squadron of news vans have shown up, and this time, it's not just Hoosier stations. I saw CNN parked in front of Beguelin's Pancake House in town and NBC, like *the* NBC, not just the local station, circling the school with their camera hanging out of the window.

There were new protestors yesterday, too, but they were banished to the cornfield across the street. They're not even *from* here. They're from that publicity-sucking church out west that does this for a living. In a way, it's almost an honor. Hey, we made the big time: national bands of bigots have arrived!

The best thing about that protest is that the *Godspell* kids came back in costume after their matinee in Terre Haute. The whole front page of our town newspaper had a picture of biblical figures clowning on the out-of-towners. Video of it ran on all the news stations last night, too, and it's still trending on Twitter.

But I admit that some of my sleeplessness was because I was . . . I'm not even sure what the right word is. *Afraid* is too big. *Anxious* is close. It's just that my bones and my body ached, hoping that this time, Alyssa would show up. That everything really would be different.

Most of my brain was fully engaged: Of course she's going to show. Everything has changed! It was just this small, silver worm of worry wriggling through me, squeaking, *But what if?! But what if?!*

As of this text, in this moment, that worm is dead. Now

I'm nervous for a whole new reason, and that's because it's prom night. My legendary suit fills me with power, and I leap at the door to throw it open when I hear an engine out front.

Oops, it's our neighbor, Mr. Martin, pulling in after his shift at the transmission factory. I wave at him, then hang from the door frame to look down the street.

I feel Barry and Dee Dee crowd in behind me, and we all watch in breathless anticipation. After approximately five million years, a dark car appears and glides toward us. It's black and sleek and looks completely out of place in our little neighborhood. It's perfect!

"Get back inside," Dee Dee says. "Act aloof. A little mysterious. Don't make her think you're desperate."

Of course, the second the limo stops, I bound out of the house. I feel like I could jump over roofs, but guess what? Gravity is still a thing! I can barely jump off the porch, and I bobble when I land. It's okay, though, because Alyssa throws herself out of the limo and we all but crash into each other in the middle of the yard.

"You look so good," she says at the same time I say, "Oh my god, you're gorgeous." We babble at each other, and honestly, I have no idea what we're saying. It's all just joyful, positive-sounding yammer, punctuated by kisses. In public! In my front yard!

I don't think cis, straight people realize how many of our kisses happen out of sight. As magical as it is to hold hands at the movies, it's incredible to hold hands on the street. A hug in a park, a nuzzle at a concert—even when you're out in Indiana, those things don't seem possible.

They are; they can be—but they're scary and dangerous, too, because you just never know what the people around you might do when they see it.

So this? This moment? I can barely breathe. I'm so drunk on sunlight and kisses bathed in them that I actually lose my balance. Alyssa catches me, and then I catch her, because we're this tangled-up, gloriously clumsy ball of pure emotion right now. There's glitter in her eye shadow and the taste of strawberry in her lipstick, and I could honestly explode from the feels right now.

"I have flowers for you," she says, gesturing at the limo. "I left them in the car."

Nobody's ever bought me flowers before. I swoon and squeeze her hands. "Wait here, I have your corsage."

Turning, I bound back into my house (nearly missing the second porch step) and almost careen into Barry. I'm so full of love right now, I could explode, and I throw my arms around him. Hugging him tight, I tell him, "You'd better save me a dance."

"As if you even have to ask," he tells me. He takes my hands and steps back, inspecting me one last time before I leave. His face is flushed, and his smile is so warm. If I didn't know better, I'd say he's on the verge of crying. He suddenly waves a hand to fan his face. "Get out of here, kid. Go get your girl."

I rise up on my toes to kiss his cheek, then turn to take the boxed corsage from Nan. She strokes my cheek, and then, like the secret monster she is, pinches it teasingly. "Your curfew is?"

"Whenever," I say, giggling.

"Very good," Nan says, and sets me free.

I look to Dee Dee for any last-minute advice, but she's face-down in pound cake and a box of tissues. I take that as a no, pack myself with zazz, and get the hell out of there. I wave and Dee Dee waves, and then I'm back out the door and down the steps to Alyssa.

The wrist corsage matches Alyssa's dress, lavender ribbon with white and lavender carnations. When I put it on her, she looks at it like I pulled out a bracelet from Tiffany or something. There are too many people tearing up right now, and it's going to make me cry, too.

"It's perfect," Alyssa says.

"I'm glad you like it," I say.

And then, because we can, because we're in the middle of my lawn, because we fought our way up a mountain to get here, because she's beautiful, because I *can*, I kiss her again and linger so long on the petal softness of her lips. I'm alive with spark and fire, and I tighten my hands on her waist.

"You ready to do this?"

"So ready," she says, her dark eyes gleaming.

And just like that, we jump in the limo and drive off into our own personal sunset—which in this case just happens to be our prom.

I never wanted much. Just to hold Alyssa's hand and walk through those gym doors and wrap my arms around her waist while she wraps hers around my neck. To dance slow to fast songs and take pictures under a hand-painted photo booth banner.

All I ever wanted was to watch the lights sparkle across her skin and share a cup of truly regrettable punch in an overheated gym.

And tonight, it happens. This is more than I dared wish for; it's epic, and there's room for everyone. Room for kids from my school. For kids from far away. For gay kids and lesbian kids, pan kids and bi kids. Ace kids are here, and trans kids, too. Nonbinary kids and cis kids. Straight kids and questioning kids and queer kids. It's a whole new family, and we're all coming out for our own big night.

We built a prom for everyone. And with those cameras watching across the street, we're showing the world that it can be done. *Godspell* escorts meet kids in the parking lot: nobody walks in alone. We stream into the gym and the marquee tents; we take selfies and fill plates and cringe as we sip the inescapable nuclear punch.

The beat of the drum urges us to take to the floor, and we do, and we move like nobody's watching. When the music blares, nobody cares who you're with. And all those miserable people across the street, still protesting? I'm sure they can feel the bass; they *have* to feel the joy.

And me? I just wanted to dance with Alyssa. Alyssa Greene, church picnic flirt and student council president. We made it here, and here we are. Under the lights, under the stars, under the disco ball, under the tents, out in the parking lot, up and down the street, everywhere in Edgewater, Indiana, and wherever you're from, too—let's go.

It's time to dance.

Broadway Score! scores a chat with Dee Dee Allen and Barry Glickman at the office of their newest endeavor, PROM FOR EVERYONE!

(cont. from page 1)

. . . a handsomely appointed office in the Flatiron, though not one that affords a view. The space is interior but bright, with photos on the wall from the prom they held last year in Edgewater, Indiana, after a gay teen there went viral with her story of discrimination. Glickman, with his trademark bombast, can hardly sit still in his Aeron chair. Allen sits on the edge of the desk, arranged and ready for a photo at any moment. Their mood can best be described as ebullient.

BS!: So you were booed at the school and the monster truck rally. What happened next?

BG: A tragedy. An absolute travesty. An abomination!

DA: They threw a fake prom for our girl and shattered her delicate little heart. We were gutted. I barely slept for days.

BS!: I can imagine. But then Emma posted that incredible video, and support came pouring in from all over the world. I know I watched it at least a hundred times.

BG: I still get verklempt thinking about it.

DA: I mean, what a star turn! She racked up millions of views practically overnight. We were going to get her booked on Kimmel, but with numbers like that . . .

BG: She did end up doing Kimmel, with Alyssa.

DA: She did. She did. [She looks away for a moment.] I can't remember the last time I did Kimmel.

BG: Fourth of never, darling.

[They laugh.]

BS!: After the video went massively viral, you put together a prom for everyone. You made Emma's wish come true.

DA: We spared no expense.

BG: Alyssa Greene, Emma's sweetheart, was the architect. Definitely the brains of the operation.

DA: But money makes the world go round, as they say! And boy, did we make it go around!

BS!: Which leads us to today. You've opened the PROM FOR EVERYONE organization. That's a nonprofit group you created to host more inclusive dances nationwide. Where will you be opening the doors next?

DA: Iowa.

BG: Idaho.

DA: Another corn-fed backwater hamlet. It's charming; they have one stoplight!

BS!: And after that?

BG: Proms across America. Everywhere Broadway goes in a bus, we'll be there right behind. And we're also working on a little something . . .

DA: We're writing our own show!

[They speak over each other, but after a moment, Glickman speaks for both of them.]

BG: We are, in fact, writing our own show. We've got most of the book done; we have feelers out for just the right composer. In our wildest dreams, Casey Nicholaw comes in for choreography and direction.

BS!: That sounds incredible. What's the show about?

DA: Our journey to Indiana and back again, the agonies, the ecstasies—we'll play ourselves, of course.

BG: We're thinking about calling it *THE PROM*!

ACKNOWLEDGMENTS

This is the happiest project I've worked on, and I'm honored that I got to be the one to bring Emma and Alyssa's side of the story to the page. That never would have happened without the amazing show that Bob Martin, Chad Beguelin, and Matthew Sklar brought to Broadway, and then trusted me with in prose; thank you.

I owe many thanks to Caitlin Kinnunen and Isabelle McCalla, Brooks Ashmanskas, and Beth Leavel, whose chemistry and performances informed every word I wrote; thank you. Heartfelt thanks to the entire team at Viking and at *The Prom* for coming together to make this book happen. It's been a privilege and an honor!

All my love and thanks to my brilliant editor Dana Leydig, who thought of me for this project, and ran through the gauntlet with me. You once said Ravenclaw and Slytherin are a very dangerous mix; we're also a mix that gets stuff done!

Finally, thank you, thank you, thank you to my agent, Jim McCarthy, who has been regularly making my dreams come true since 2012. Thank you for this, thank you for everything we've already done together, and thank you for the future I see more clearly because of you.

—Saundra Mitchell

We would like to thank Casey Nicholaw for his leadership, Dori Berinstein and Bill Damaschke for their intestinal fortitude, Jack Viertel for his cleverness, Izzy McCalla for her humanity, Brooks Ashmanskas for his audacity, Beth Leavel for her belt, Angie Schworer for her legs, Chris Sieber for his hair, Caitlin Kinnunen for her overall, unwavering Caitlin-ness, and Saundra Mitchell for connecting with our show so deeply, and filling in the blanks so brilliantly. Additionally, we would like to thank Cait Hoyt and Erin Malone for making the deal and Dana Leydig and Eileen Kreit from Penguin Random House for making it real.

—Bob Martin, Chad Beguelin, & Matthew Sklar

The producers of *The Prom* musical, Dori Berinstein, Bill Damaschke, and Jack Lane, would like to acknowledge Broadway show conceiver Jack Viertel; director/choreographer Casey Nicholaw; show creators Bob Martin, Chad Beguelin, and Matthew Sklar; the spectacular cast of *The Prom*; and our entire *Prom* family behind the curtain. We'd also like to thank general managers Aaron Lustbader, Lane Marsh, and Nick Ginsberg, and our *Prom* co-producers and investors. A million thanks also to our house and company management team, including Marc Borsak and Alex Wolfe as well as Kenny Nunez and the crew at the Longacre Theater. Thank you to Clint Bond, Meghan Dixon, and the team at On the Rialto; Polk & Co., including Matt Polk, Colgan McNeil, and Kelly Stotmeister; the Situation team, led by Damian Bazadona, Pippa Bexon, and Rian Durham; and our AKA family, including Scott Moore and Jacob Matsumiya. And a special thanks to the wonderful Rose Polidoro.

·····················➤

Turn the page for more about
the musical, the show creators,
and the cast of *The Prom*!

Notes from Co-Writer Bob Martin on *The Prom*: the musical

May 2010. Chad, Matt, Casey Nicholaw, and I meet with Jack Viertel, venerable producer/writer/artistic director and all around musical theatre guru. Casey has brought us here to the Jujamcyn offices on West 44th street because Jack has an idea he wants to pitch. "A small town girl tries to take her same sex partner to the prom, but the school won't let her. A bunch of Broadway performers come down to fix things. They make it much worse." I'm paraphrasing, but that's how I remember it. Jack pitched us, in a few words, the premise for a rollicking musical comedy with heart; a show rooted in a harsh sociopolitical reality, but littered with ridiculous characters doing stupid things. We said yes.

November 2018. We open on Broadway. Quite a bit happened in those eight years. Yes, a musical was written and rewritten, workshopped, choreographed, staged, and re-staged. But more significantly, the sociopolitical context in which the show was conceived changed dramatically. There was actually a point early on in development when we thought that the show might no longer be relevant. Lots of progress was being made, particularity in the area of LGBTQIA+ rights, and there was a general sense of optimism in the air. Well, incidents of the kind described in the libretto continued to happen, and then a contentious, bitter election split the country in half. Suddenly people found themselves on either side of a vast, unbridgeable cultural divide. Our show seemed more relevant than ever.

Perhaps that's why the army of people involved in shepherding *The Prom* from premise to Broadway show are so passionate about it. We are all desperately in need of hope. We all feel Emma's pain when she realizes that the whole town has conspired against her, we all cry when Barry dances with joy in his motel room after being told he is finally going to prom, and we all struggle with Mrs. Greene as she tries to see her daughter for who she is instead of who she wants her to be. The cast, the crew, everyone around the production table, were all a mess after every run-through, because the show is filled with painfully relatable truths. In the end, *The Prom* is about how a small, rickety bridge is built in Edgewater, Indiana, between two sides of the culture wars. We hope that those who see *The Prom*, and those who listen to the recording, will laugh and cry and get inspired to build something of their own.

—Bob Martin

The following are excerpts from an interview conducted by cast member Josh Lamon with the creative team of Bob Martin, Chad Beguelin, and Matthew Sklar during a launch event for *The Prom* in New York City.

JOSH LAMON: From your perspective as a lyricist, as co-book writer, what has the show been like going through the changes from day one around the table, to the labs and Atlanta, to now?

CHAD BEGUELIN: It's changed so much. I think the biggest change, I mean, we're constantly tweaking it and working on it, but the world sort of changed. We were thinking that the world has gotten so much more accepting and wondering if this was as relevant, and then the election happened, and it suddenly became so important and so relevant. All of these things we thought we were past—suddenly the show took on this new level of immediacy. I couldn't predict that would happen. It's been a great journey and having this great cast has been so much fun for all of us to write for. It's been great.

We were really concentrating on this last pass of the script and the score to make sure that we didn't show the other side to be completely caricatures. We wanted to make sure that everyone was dealt with fairly—these people just had different beliefs and they had to work through them throughout the show.

JOSH LAMON: One of my favorite things about *The Prom* is that it is hilarious but also serious. We are talking about an actual story that happened.

BOB MARTIN: Several actually. It's based on several incidents that happened and continue to happen across this wonderful country.

JOSH LAMON: What was it like tackling the comedy versus the serious material?

BOB MARTIN: I like the combination of making potentially unpalatable truths easier to take when they're surrounded by people like you. You're the sugar that makes the medicine go down easily. I think what's really interesting about this show is that people cry, but it's an extremely funny show. As you can see there's a mixture of very broad comedy and the very grounded, serious story at the heart of it all. It was remarkable to have people come up to us after the show and be so moved. I had this woman come with her head down and confess that she was the mother depicted in the story, with tears in her eyes making this confession to us. I think it is a very moving show for that very reason.

JOSH LAMON: What was unique about this process for you?

MATTHEW SKLAR: Well, it's one of the first times I've ever really written something completely original from the ground up. Anything else I've ever written has had some kind of source material. So this was a great opportunity, and I just love working with these guys [Chad Beguelin and Bob Martin] and with Casey [Nicholaw]. I think we all bring out the best in each other. The story is just so moving. Once we started outlining the story, seeing where it was going, and figuring out where the songs would go, it felt like both sides complemented each other—the comedy and the dramatic aspect of it. It's been a joy to work on.